OUR FATHER,

Frank

THE STORY OF A PRIEST, THE WOMAN HE LOVED AND THE SONS THEY LEFT BEHIND

Jack

SORRY FOR THE DELAY!
CALL MY BROTHER WHEN
YOU GET THIS.

LET ME
KNOW
WHAT
YOU
THINK

[signature]

JOSEPH CHAMBERLIN

9-29-15

JOE@PRAXISMEDIATION.COM

ISBN: 1439250170
ISBN-13: 9781439250174

THIS WORK IS
DEDICATED TO

IDA AND MIKE CHAMBERLIN
MY MOM AND MY DAD
AND TO MY SONS
CHRISTOPHER AND JOHN

ACKNOWLEDGEMENTS

Deedra Jungers for inspiring me to write;
Brian Rafkin for helping me be still to write;
Leslie Kleban for insisting that I rewrite;
Donna McMahon for a careful, final reading,
and
Michael Mark Evans
for
The financial support to bring the writing to print.

"God utters me like a word containing
a partial thought of himself."
New Seeds of Contemplation
Thomas Merton

MORNING

The almost drained bottle of Pikesville Rye sat on the table between two empty glasses next to an ashtray full of cigarette butts.

"You always hurt the one you love…" softly drifted into the now still, dark room from the radio on the nearby dresser.

Across the room Frank McGowan strained to see the time on his wristwatch. The more he awakened to where he was, the more a sense of urgency seized him. He rolled to one side of the bed so as not to disturb the woman still deep in sleep. He sat and stared at her for a moment, then smiled before turning to other things.

As he stretched out his arm to take his trousers from the chair next to the bed, he caught himself whispering along with the words on the radio, "You always take the sweetest rose and push it until the petals fall."

He lingered for a moment on the side of the bed. Standing, he reached for his shirt and sweater as he moved to look out the window onto the dark street before he took leave of this sanctuary. Almost to the door, he stopped for one more glance at the slumbering figure.

1

As he slowly opened the door, he reached out to pick up his Roman collar beside the white starched nurse's cap on the dresser.

"Good morning, Father," rose the voice from the bed as the woman sat up and clicked on a lamp.

"Oh, I didn't mean to wake you, Susan," he said ignoring her formal greeting.

"I am sure the Mills Brothers appreciate your knowing the words to their song.

When will I see you again?" she asked, holding her thin face on her hand, allowing her long brown hair to hang loosely down her arm. While the sheet covered most of her breast, enough remained exposed to hold his eye for another moment.

"The next time you come to church or I visit the hospital," he explained.

"Remember, I work on the third floor," she said.

She murmured to herself, "Men, they're all alike. Whether they wear a stethoscope or a cross." Her sleepy blue eyes barely open, she thought about getting out of bed, but instead pulled the covers over her head.

She lay there and remembered the first time they slept together.

He was a new face at the hospital. And new faces were always welcome, especially if they were men. The work was as challenging as she had hoped it would be. What had become difficult was being a single woman. There were always doctors to go out with, but their attention span and commitment for more than a few hours were, well, she sometimes felt like she was just another case to them.

That morning she had come into Mr. Brown's room to see a man in a clerical suit sitting at the patient's bedside reading from a book. She had seen other clerical men reading similar books, but this one was different. He did not look up.

Then, as she approached, he looked up and smiled.

"Good morning, nurse," he said, and went back to his book.

"Good morning, Father," she responded.

"Am I in your way?" the priest asked.

"No Father," she said as she walked to the other side of Mr. Brown's bed.

The man appeared to be sleeping. She gently took the patient's wrist and as the priest looked at his watch he looked up at her, then back to his book.

"Do you want me to leave?" the priest asked not quite sure what she was about to do.

"No," she smiled.

With this the cleric stood and said, "I think I'll go have a smoke."

Mr. Brown stirred and from his sleepy weakened state noticed the two of them.

"Am I interrupting you two?" he asked.

The pair, turning to the voice, smiled and said in unison, "No."

"How are you today, Mr. Brown?" the nurse asked.

"Well, not so bad…for someone who is dying." He ended his sentence with an air of surrender.

"What makes you say that?" she asked.

"Please, nurse, I have lived long enough to know that I won't be here much longer," he said.

He was dying and everyone, including the nurse, knew. He had been a miner for more than twenty-five years. This coupled with the two-plus packs of cigarettes he smoked every day had blackened his lungs. Then there was the recent fall that broke his hip so that he no longer got the exercise to keep enough air in his lungs to prevent their collapse.

"Would you like Father to stay, Mr. Brown?" asked the nurse. "I'm sorry, Father, I don't know your name."

"Frank," he answered. "Father Frank McGowan. I'm the new Associate at Saint Patrick's."

"Father Frank is here almost every day," explained Mr. Brown. "He brings me communion and has been trying to get me... ready..." His voice trailed off into a prolonged rough cough.

"Now, Mr. Brown," began the nurse reaching for a glass of water and moving to the side of the man's bed, "take it easy. What is he getting you ready for?"

"My final ride around town," Mr. Brown said with a smile of sorts as he returned the glass of water to the nurse.

He was referring to a custom where the funeral procession drove around town after leaving the church to pass the deceased person's house on the way to the cemetery.

"Really, Mr. Brown, I don't know if we are at that point," said Father Frank trying to play down Mr. Brown's forecast.

"Go on Nurse, tell him you've been here with the doctors," said Mr. Brown, looking to the nurse for confirmation.

The nurse, standing at his side, reached down to be sure he was comfortable and said, "Mr. Brown, you're not going anywhere today."

Mr. Brown smiled again and looked to Father McGowan.

"I'll be back tomorrow, Mr. Brown. Let me give you a blessing," the priest said as he stepped to the foot of the man's bed. Raising his right hand he began, "*In nomine Patri*" and moving his hand in the air from right to left, "*et Fili et Spiritui Sancti.*"

The patient moved his fingers from his forehead to his heart, then to his left shoulder, then to his right shoulder before putting his hands together saying, "Amen."

All the while the nurse stood silently.

Out in the hall, Father Frank walked to the waiting room where he sat down. He pulled out a pack of Camels and lit one. After a few minutes he crushed the still burning cigarette into the others in the ashtray and stood to leave. The nurse from Mr. Brown's room approached.

"Hello," she said with a smile.

"Hello," said Father Frank. "I did not get your name back there in Mr. Brown's room."

Pointing to the name plate on her white uniform blouse, "Susan," she added as if to be sure he got it. "Will you be here for awhile, Father? I don't think Mr. Brown has much longer."

"Well," began the priest, " I have a few other patients to visit. I can come back after I see them. I did administer last rites to Mr. Brown twice this past month."

"What are last rites?" the nurse asked.

"It's a Catholic sacrament we administer to people who are dying," he explained. "It helps get them ready."

"Get ready? For that final ride around town?" she interrupted him wanting to know. She had seen the ritual during her time at the hospital, but she had never felt comfortable asking.

"Get ready to meet the Lord," he said, realizing she probably was not Catholic. "To die."

"I'm sorry, Father, I didn't know. Thank you."

Susan was pleased with his taking the time to explain the "last rites." She was not really sure what "last rites" was. But she was sure that it did appear to do something for Mr. Brown.

As the two parted they smiled at each other.

Mr. Brown died later that day and Father Frank did return to administer last rites, again.

Susan watched quietly as Father Frank stood over the man. A purple cloth draped around his neck as he read from his black book. She was impressed with his presence at the side of a man who was now dead. He was as attentive to him as if he were still alive. Too many times there in the hospital, once death had occurred, everyone, especially the doctors, were on to someone else.

They talked often after that day. They drank coffee together. She often asked him to stop in to see someone she thought might benefit from talking with him.

On a Saturday afternoon several weeks later, a young boy who had been hit by a car was brought into the emergency room. There was blood everywhere. The doctors were preparing to perform emergency surgery to find the source of the bleeding.

Susan was relieved to see Father Frank when she walked into the emergency room. He was putting the purple cloth around his neck when a woman, the boy's mother, started screaming at him.

"Get away from him! I don't want you near him!"

Father Frank stopped and stood still as the woman continued to rant.

"How can there be a God? What kind of God would let this happen to my son!?"

Father Frank stepped closer and reached out to the woman. She lunged at him with both fists clenched to strike him. As she did, she collapsed into his arms.

Susan and another nurse took the fallen woman from the priest.

Father Frank stood at the boy's side. He heard the boy's breath fading. As he reached out his arm to anoint the boy's forehead, the boy turned his head toward him. The youth said not a word. Their eyes met. The boy sighed, turned his head away, and died.

"Why?" thought Father Frank.

This was not the first time Father Frank had anointed a child. It was the first time, however, he wondered "why?"

Soon afterward, as Father Frank sat in the hospital's small chapel staring at a candle on a plain table that served as an altar, Susan came in and sat beside him.

"You look like you could use a drink," she said.

"What makes you say that?" he asked.

"I'm a nurse."

Out on the street, Father Frank walked two blocks to the hospital parking lot. At his '42 Buick, he paused a second to breathe in the morning. He opened the car door and within three minutes he pulled into his destination. He parked the car alongside the two other cars. Hoping no one saw him, Father Frank made his way down three steps counting *one, two, three* to himself. He felt a mixture of satisfaction from where he had come and a profound angst about where he was going there in the parking lot of St. Patrick's Roman Catholic Church in Cumberland, Maryland.

The United States was at war this October morning of 1944. Tucked in the mountainous hills of Appalachia, Cumberland was less than one hundred miles from Pittsburgh and even farther from Baltimore, the largest city in Maryland and from where Father Frank had been reassigned. Even though it was remote, the town was engaged in the struggle, too. Most of the eligible young men of the town were in uniform, on battlefields in Europe or the Pacific. The first hint of blue cracked the dark sky. The midnight shifts of those who stayed home to mold tires for fighter planes at the Kelly tire plant, mine the coal that would soon be in Pittsburgh to become the steel for hulls of war ships or the metal casings of shells, were less than an hour from ending. Local barkeeps prepared for their after-work arrivals.

Inside the sacristy of St. Patrick's, Frank put his coat on the rack near the door. He moved to a large oak cupboard and, after removing his sweater, slid it into the corner of the counter. He dragged a book across from the other side of the large flat surface. Soon, he was reciting prayers as he dressed with the vestments to say Mass.

Lifting a rectangle of cloth with thin chords hanging down, he laid this amice on his back and crossed his chest with the two thin white chords. He reached behind his back to pull and tie the chords about his waist. As he tied it he tried to focus on why he was there. Then, he lifted a white alb from the table and pulled it over his head. He was now covered in the white robe and he began to feel more like a priest, a person anointed to lead the community in prayer, a person of spiritual substance. Next, he lifted the stole, a long green strip of clothe, put it to his lip and draped it over his neck. Lifting the cincture, a white rope, he wrapped it around his waist being sure to enclose the stole. He looped and tightened it, tugging on it a bit more than usual, as if to administer himself some discomfort. Some pain. Punishment.

As Father Frank finished vesting, a young man of about ten emerged from the door leading out to the altar.

"Good morning, Father," came the soft respectful voice from the boy dressed in a black cassock and starch less white surplice.

"Good morning, Jack," was all Father Frank could say into the mirror as he finished straightening his vestments.

"Father," Jack began sheepishly, "may I ask you a question?"

"Sure Jack."

"How many candles today?" asked Jack, relieved to have the question out.

"How many candles?"

"How many candles do I light today?" Jack asked.

The look on Jack's face told the priest that the young man was perplexed.

"Well, Jack," the priest turned to look at the boy, "it's not Sunday and it is not a holy day or high mass or a funeral mass when we light sex, *six*...."

The priest caught himself quick enough so that the boy did not hear the miscue. "So it will be a low mass. Two candles."

Lifting the green chasuble from the oak counter, he put it over his head and, moving to the mirror, straightened it and mumbled what might have been a prayer, almost aloud, to himself as he pinned the maniple to his white sleeve.

Should I really be doing this? Oh my God I am heartily sorry...a perfect act of contrition. I'll say a perfect act of contrition. It is a weekday mass, so no need for a sermon. Recite the prayers, read the Epistle, Gospel, consecrate the bread and wine, distribute it, and get on with my day.

"Let's go, Jack," Father Frank said as he lifted the chalice covered with the paten tucked in the burse beneath the green chalice veil. The two moved out onto the altar to the gazes of twenty or so parishoners, mostly women, who came for morning Mass.

What happened? he asked himself as he placed the chalice on the altar and bowed and turned and walked down the steps to begin the prayers.

"*Introibo ad altare Dei*, (I will go unto the altar of God)," Father Frank started after crossing himself.

9

"*Ad Deum qui laetificat juventutem meam*, (the God who was a joy in my youth)," responded Jack.

Maybe it has something to do with getting older. He was the God of gladness and joy when I was younger, when I felt more gladness and joy.

"*Confiteor Deo omnipotenti* (I confess to Almighty God) *quia peccavi nimis cogitatione verbo, et opere* (I have sinned exceedingly in thought, word and deed)," Father Frank struck his breast three times saying. "*Mea Culpa, Mea Culpa, Mea Maxima Culpa* (through my fault, through my fault, through my most grievous fault)."

He recited each of these words slowly, hoping that they would do something for him.

As he finished his prayers there at the foot of the altar, he took the three steps—"*one, two, three*" again to himself—and bowed before the altar. He then looked at the book, raised his hands, and read the Latin words. These words moved the Mass.

Father Frank only turned to face the gathered to bless them or invite them to pray. It was a weekday. No need to have to look out onto the faces of the gathered. Many were mothers with sons in the struggle on battlefields far away. Most listened to his every word, looking only at him. Others followed along with their prayer books and some fingered their rosary beads while following his every movement.

As he read the prayers, he tried to get behind the words, their meanings. He remembered as a seminarian looking at some of his classmates and wondering if they were in a trance. They appeared mesmerized. And, at times, he too felt himself taken, caught up in trying to be with, understand, and live the words he was reading. He read from the book on the altar that the day's Epistle was from a letter from Paul to the Church of Corinth. He read from the first letter Chapter 9, verses: 24-10, 5.

Although the words were in Latin he thought of them in English:

Brethren: Do you know that those who run in a race, all indeed run, but one receives the prize? So run as to obtain it.

Now, who here will receive the prize? he thought to himself. He continued to think to himself while reading, *For so long I thought it was me. I thought because of who I am and what I do, I would receive the prize. Now, I am not too sure. These faces sitting before me, listening to words they do not understand. Perhaps it is they who will receive it.*

"*Dominus Vobis cum* (the Lord be with you)," he chanted toward the crowd.

"*Et cum spiritu tuo* (and with your spirit)," Jack said clearly and, at these words, everyone rose to their feet.

The Gospel, the word of God for this morning is from Matthew, Chapter 20, verse 1-16, the parable of the workers in the vineyard. All received the same pay for varying amounts of work. And then when those who had worked all day realized they were receiving the same as those who had come in at the eleventh hour, they complained. In response, the master explained, "Even so the last shall be first, and the first last; *for many are called, but few are chosen.*"

These words hung above the chapel in the seminary, in Latin, intended for those who entered there and stayed there long enough. These words stayed with him as he went about the rest of Mass.

Now, now, he knew all the words and he knew them well. Each reminded him of where he had been and where he had come to.

"*Lavabo*…I wash my hands in innocence and I go around your altar, O Lord," hoping they would become innocent.

Father Frank held the chalice out to Jack, and the altar boy poured wine from the cruet into the chalice. He almost asked him to go and fetch the whole bottle. When it was time for the water, he had Jack pour just enough to cover the wine as if there was a requirement to meet.

As he prepared for the consecration, Father Frank grew more uncomfortable. He was perspiring. If not so much from the thought of what he was doing and what he had been doing, as from the drinks. *Was it four or five?* He wondered how many he had the night before.

Leaning over the host he whispered aloud, "*Hoc est enim Corpus meum* (This is my body)."

Lifting the bread above his head, he heard again the sound of the bells breaking the morning silence.

"*Hic est enim Calix Sanguinis mei, nove et aeterni testamenti; mysterium fidei; quipro vobis at pro multis effundetur in remissionem pecatorum.* (For this is the chalice of my Blood of the new and eternal covenant: the mystery of faith: which shall be shed for you and for many unto the forgiveness of sins."

He gave His life; shed His blood so that we might live, he thought to himself. *And what is that life to be about?* Now he was not sure, sure if these words, which had been so sacred to him, meant anything to him anymore.

He remembered the first time he said these words the day after his ordination at his first Mass. He had been saying them in his room up on the third floor of St. Mary's Seminary in Roland Park, a more pastoral part of Baltimore city. It was quiet up there in that room looking out over the neighborhood he had come to call home. The long walks in the tree lined streets and the large lawn that stretched from the seminary building out to the woods. He would be alone in his room and wonder about how these words would be different after the Bishop laid his hands on him.

That Saturday morning often came to him at these moments. He remembered the Bishop calling him from his prostrate position on the marble floor there in the Basilica of the Assumption on Charles Street just across from Calvert Hall College, the Christian Brothers' High School where he taught religion to young men who could afford the sort of private school that he only dreamed of attending.

He lay there, feet outstretched, hoping that his worn left shoe would make it one more day.

"Francis Joseph McGowan," came the Bishop's voice, loud and clear as if he were the only person in the church.

This was the time and place he had waited so long for, his place on the cool marble floor, his face resting in the fresh white alb covering his crossed arms. He was about to be ordained a priest in the Roman Catholic Church.

As he lay there inhaling the fresh clean starch smell he could almost see his grandmother hanging damp white sheets, fresh from the wash, on the clothes line that stretched from one end of their tiny yard to the other. There he lay, next to the others, lying as still as he could, across the street from the newly built Pratt Library amidst the slow hum of Saturday morning traffic that competed with birds announcing another Baltimore spring day.

"*Adsum* (I am Here)," came Frank's response. Here, present, and willing to take the next, seventh step to Tabor, the step which entitles me, allows me to forgive sins, bind marriages, welcome the newly born, prepare the dying, and, most important,

13

consecrate the bread and wine within the Mass, the highest of the Roman Catholic rituals.

As he genuflected and turned to leave the altar this October morning, he glanced out into the almost empty church and noticed a woman, a young, attractive woman sitting mid way down the sanctuary. He could feel her eyes.

Back in the safety of the vestry he walked to the counter and put down the covered chalice. Jack returned to the altar to extinguish the candles. As Frank began to remove the vestments his mind drifted again, back to those days, those wonderful days just before he was ordained, when he anticipated how right everything would be, once he was ordained.

"Father...Father," Jack's voice called him back to this Wednesday morning almost thirteen years after that Saturday morning. He looked to his left to see the altar boy.

"Yes, Jack, what is it?" he sighed as he removed the cincture from his waist.

"There is a lady out in the church..."

Agitated, Father Frank interrupted, "There were lots of ladies out in the church, Jack."

(*In fact*, he thought to himself, *there were only ladies in the church.*)

"But Father, this lady asked to talk with you," Jack explained.

"Did she say what it was about?" asked the priest as he lifted the chasuble over his head.

"No," replied the boy.

The priest tried to look out into the church without being seen to size up how much time this might take. An older lady with nothing to do today could be looking for an answer to a question that would take more than a few minutes to answer. A younger woman might want an opportunity to talk about a wedding or check when confessions were and that would not keep him from the cigarette that was most on his mind at this moment.

"Tell her I'll be right there," the priest said lifting the wrinkled moist alb over his head and noticing it might best be placed in the laundry.

As he tossed the alb into the nearby wicker basket, he looked across the large oak counter for his Roman collar. With collar in place he moved to the coat rack then remembered that he had left his sweater on the oak cabinet. Turning back, he grabbed the grey mass of wool, lifted it close to inhale what remained of last night's encounter, and pulled it on as he walked out into the church.

A few steps into the sacristy he noticed the woman, a solitary figure, away from the others who knelt praying quietly. It was the lady whose eyes he had felt and then he remembered: he had visited this woman in the hospital about a month ago. *Now, if I can only remember her name,* he said to himself as he genuflected to the altar and walked down the three steps into the main church.

Approaching her, she stood and he reached out his hand to her. "Hello, I am Father Frank."

Her hand was soft and warm, a little shaky.

"Good morning, Father. Do you remember me?" she said nervously. "You visited me in the hospital last month."

"Yes, I remember you…," he replied, hoping to recall her name.

"My name is Eileen."

"Yes, Eileen," he said calmly. She seemed upset. "You look… well. Your recovery is complete from the surgery?"

"Yes. Yes, Father, I am feeling much better."

"Well, Eileen, Jack told me you wanted to talk with me."

"Jack?" she asked.

"Jack. I'm sorry. The altar boy you spoke with."

He looked over at her face. He found himself looking beyond her eyes, beyond the clear blue of her moist eyes to a grayness of the person who stood before him. The more he stared, the more difficult he found it to pull his eyes away from hers.

"I would like to talk with you about something," she said.

"Something?" he asked. "Can you be more specific?"

"Well, I'd rather not say here," she said looking down and away, breaking the connection of their staring eyes.

"Okay, why don't you come and see me at the rectory?"

"When?" she wanted to know.

"I'm there most days and evenings, except Thursday. That's my day off."

"Can I come in on Friday evening?"

"Yes, how about 7:30?" he said hesitatingly.

"That'll be ok," she said not moving.

"Are you going to be alright?" he asked, not sure if he should leave her.

"Yes, I'll be fine," she replied. "I have to go now, so I'll see you at 7:30 on Friday evening."

She moved slowly out of the pew as he walked up the aisle through the opened altar rail to the foot of the altar. As he rose from genuflecting to the altar, he turned to see her walking slowly down the center aisle. He stopped to watch her walk away as if the weight of the world was on her shoulders.

He thought to himself, *She's so very pretty and yet so very sad.*

DINNER

That Friday, as he went to pour a second drink in the Pastor's living room, Frank remembered he had an appointment. The Pastor was Monsignor Robert Lynch, a simple country priest who set directions with clear rules and no compromises. His church was the true church, and he was the man in charge. Every Friday evening he invited his priests into his living room for drinks before dinner. Tonight they were all there: Father O'Toole, Father Wise, and Father Frank.

"Never have more than one drink if you have an evening appointment," Frank remembered Father Coyle, now Bishop Coyle, telling him on that Friday night before his ordination in May 1931. So, instead, he made his way to the kitchen with an empty glass.

Friday night at the rectory was fish night. The cook, Bertha, one of the few Negroes in Cumberland, was an excellent cook. Fish was one of her specialties. She made her own breading of bread crumbs and special, spicy seasoning through which she dredged the fish before pan frying the fillets in an iron skillet she brought from home. It made the bland, nondescript fish almost a treat. Most of the priests took a courteous if not altogether warm liking to Bertha, who asked the friendlier clerics to call her Bert.

Frank often brought his glass to the kitchen, not so much out of politeness as an excuse to get out of what he came to call "Friday night with the Pastor." This gathering of priests reminded him of the old "Rules with the Rex" sessions during high school at St. Gregory's seminary because the Rector, who did not particularly like having high school aged boys about, thought they needed a little reminding of seminary's rules. Frank often stopped in the kitchen to say hello to Bert. Thin and very sober and quiet, she liked to cook what they thought she should cook. So she prepared lots of meat and potatoes and deep fried things. She cooked them, but seldom ate any herself. She had a bad stomach and ate light and often drank buttermilk. She didn't really mind taking care of her "boys," as she referred to them. For the most part, they were polite if not always friendly. Except for Father Frank, there was very little interaction between her and her "boys."

"What's on the menu, Bert?" he asked as he set the glass on the kitchen sink.

"Do you really have to ask? It's Friday night. Fried fish and French fries, plus some of my special green beans."

"Oh, those green beans, those very special green beans that have that wonderful..."

"Don't say another word," she chimed in.

"Do I smell biscuits?" He moved to the oven with a towel in hand to check on their progress. With the oven open, he counted the browning biscuits. "Thirteen, you have enough for the last supper."

"I always fix enough food as if I was cooking for Jesus. And you, you better get in there before Monsignor sends one of the others looking for you." She shushed him toward the dining room door.

"Okay. Okay, I'll go," he said.

Walking through the door from the kitchen to the dining room was like crossing into another world; from a shore of warmth and consideration to an icy sea. It was visceral. The Pastor, Monsignor Lynch, sat there with his arms outstretched on to the table as the others sat, silently, waiting, for what exactly was anyone's guess.

"Good of you to join us, Father," said the monsignor.

"Sorry Monsignor," the newly arrived priest said as he moved to his place, opposite Monsignor at the other end of the table.

"Perhaps you would like Bertha to join us?" asked Monsignor. His words dripped with sarcasm, something he was quite skilled in.

"Well…," Father Frank began, paused, then decided to stop altogether.

"You were saying Father?" retorted the monsignor.

"Nothing, Monsignor, nothing," said Father O'Toole trying to end the exchange.

"Let us pray then…," began Monsignor.

"Lord, we are thankful for this day, this bread and the hands that have prepared it. May we always use these gifts as you use us, in your service."

"Amen," responded the three other priests.

Before the amen was finished, Monsignor had lifted, rung, and replaced the small bell that sat just above his plate. He was reaching for his wine glass to raise in quest of someone to fill it as if he was on the altar preparing for the Eucharist. In an almost flawless motion, Father Wise, the priest to his right, had the bottle of white wine poised and ready to pour as Bertha brought in two full dishes. One platter was filled with breaded fillets of fish and French fried potatoes while the other, a bowl, was filled to the brim with green beans wafting a familiar fragrance of something, which, by the look on the face of at least one of the priests, had piqued his curiosity.

As she placed one then the other of the two dishes in front of Monsignor, Father O'Toole commented, more to himself than to the others.

"Do I smell bacon?"

"Shh..." replied Father Wise, one of the more senior priests.

"Father," said Monsignor, hearing the comment, "It is Friday. We do not eat meat or anything cooked with meat. So, you must be mistaken."

So began dinner on Friday night at St. Patrick's Rectory. Few words were spoken other than those in response to Monsignor's comments on the crispness of the French fries or the pleasant flavor of the green beans.

"Father Frank," Monsignor began, "I see you have an appointment tonight, Friday night."

"Yes, Monsignor," answered Frank hoping there would be no more said.

"Does that mean you won't be joining us for cards?" Monsignor wanted to know.

"No, Monsignor, I plan to come after my appointment," answered Frank, while actually he wanted to say something quite different.

"Father O'Toole, will we be seeing you this evening?" Monsignor asked.

"Yes, Monsignor, I wouldn't miss it," replied the young cleric.

"What about you, Father Wise?" Monsignor made his way around the table.

"I'll be there Monsignor," he answered, recanting any thought of not going.

"Good," Monsignor said, summarizing the line-up. "With Father Conner joining us we should have a good game. See you all at 8:00." He looked at Father Frank, "And what time will you be joining us, Father?"

"I should be there by 9:00, Monsignor," Frank said to reassure the elder.

With this, the four of them continued their supper, each having a second portion of green beans to avoid any serious conversation. Soon, Monsignor sipped the last of his wine, sat the empty glass on the table and stood, placing his crumpled linen napkin on his chair. Noticing at least one of the priests about to stand, Monsignor extended his hand to the group, assuring him he did not have to rise.

"Stay. Finish your dinner," he implored. "Bertha surely has a treat for you for dessert."

As Monsignor left the room, the priests offered up an almost audible sigh of relief.

THE APPOINTMENT

She spent more than her usual amount of time getting ready.

Should I wear the black dress? No, too formal. The print? No. Don't like the way it looks on me. Not that she had lots to pick from; it was that she wanted to look good, no matter how bad she felt inside. She so often felt out of sorts. There was about her a sadness, a sadness she was always trying to cover with make-up, a pretty dress, a witty remark.

As always, whatever she did, she made the sadness attractive.

This is it. This is the one I'll wear, she thought, holding a black dress with the purple flowers against her thin frame.

He sat reading his breviary, wanting to finish the evening prayer knowing that he would probably not have time later. *Now what time is she coming? I wonder what she wants to talk about. Nothing else to do on a Friday night? Probably a failing marriage. Probably needs to hear that she has to stick it out. Make it work. Remind her that she took a vow before God. 7:30. That's when she's coming.*

As she stood before the mirror, running the brush through her long black hair, she asked herself, *I wonder how old he is?*

He lifted his head from the Psalm, *I wonder how old she is?*

What kind of earrings do you wear to go see a priest? she asked herself as she fingered the dish on her bureau.

Whether it was the time of day or the drink before dinner, Father Frank dozed off to find himself in a dream.

"May I have this dance?" he was asking the lady with nothing else to do on a Friday night. They were in a crowded room, a grand room lit by candles. He was in a blue uniform with a chest full of medals. She wore a magnificent purple satin dress with a single strand of pearls around her neck, and pearl earrings.

As she curtsied to accept, she stretched out her white-gloved hand and, as he reached to take it into his, she looked into his eyes. He returned the gaze and the two found themselves effortlessly moving to the rhythm of a waltz. She smelled of lilacs.

As they danced, he looked down at the marble floor to see a Marian mosaic.

Knock!

Knock!

It was the second knock that called him back to his rectory room.

"Father!" a gentle, yet firm voice came from the other side of the door. "Father, are you awake?"

"Yes," sitting up and wiping a bit of drool from the corner of his mouth.

"Yes, I'm awake."

"Someone is here to see you."

"Okay, tell them I'll be right there."

Stirring himself, he stood and walked into the bathroom. Quickly he splashed some water on his face, brushed his teeth, and after running a comb through his thinning grayish-black hair, flicked off the light and walked out of the bathroom humming a waltz.

She sat on the edge of the chair clutching her handbag. Gazing about the room she noticed the things on the desk in front of her. She smiled as she glanced at the name plate on the desk, FR. Francis J. McGowan. "FR," she thought to herself, " FR? What?" she wondered. "That must be for Father."

As her eyes moved about the room she noticed a picture on the wall. Standing she reluctantly took a step toward it. Approaching the Madonna and child, she smiled.

"Good evening," came the voice still in her memory.

Turning, she continued her gaze, now at him, as he crossed the room to her.

"Good evening, Father," she responded with a smile.

"I see you noticed our painting. It's one of my favorites. Of course, I do not know if they ever sat for a portrait," he said, attempting to lighten the moment.

She did not respond.

"Please, sit down," he directed her back to the chair where she had been sitting.

He had walked around to the other side of the desk and, as he pulled the chair out to seat himself, he spoke her name.

"Eileen. Did I say it correctly? I often confuse Ellen with Eileen."

The sound of her name coming from him pleased her.

"Yes, that's right, my name is Eileen, Eileen Elizabeth," she said, leaving off her last name.

"Oh, forgive me," Father Frank said, rising from the chair and taking the few steps from behind the desk, "Let me take your coat."

She stood and began removing her coat. As she did, he came closer and he noticed her fragrance, purple lilacs, and for an instant he was back in his dream.

"Can I get you a cup of coffee?"

"No thanks."

"Tea?"

"Thank you, but no, I'm fine," she said, sitting back down and carefully folding her thin unadorned hands on her lap.

Walking to the coat rack, her perfume wafted from her coat and filled his senses. He wanted to pull the coat to his face.

"Now, Eileen," the priest started, returning to his chair and trying to focus on what he was supposed to be doing, "what brings you to St. Patrick's on a Friday night?"

"Well, Father, I really don't know where to begin," she replied, struggling for words.

"That's okay," he reassured her. "Just try to tell me what's on your mind."

"It's about my marriage."

"What about your marriage?" he asked, reaching for a cigarette and the lighter that he had put on the desk when he sat down. He offered her one. She declined.

"Something is wrong? I don't know if that is the right word, *wrong*."

There was silence.

"Eileen, I know this must be difficult," he tried, saying words that he had said many times before, "it must be difficult to talk about your marriage, but it may help. Tell me a little about yourself."

"I was born here in Cumberland and lived in Barton."

"Up George's Creek?" he asked to keep the conversation going.

"Yes," she said. "is there another?"

"Not that I know of," he responded. "When were you married?"

"Twelve years ago."

"Where?"

"Here."

"So, you were married here in, let's see that would have been, 1932?"

"Yes, 1932. June 1, 1932."

"What is your husband's name?"

"Bill."

"Why did you and Bill marry?"

A blush came over her face and, realizing she was in the presence of a priest although not in the confessional, she felt a certain ease with having to confess, again.

"I got pregnant."

He did not wince or say a word, only continued to look at her, with eyes that said that it was okay. This reaction was new to her as most others looked judgingly at her.

"I became pregnant with our daughter and Bill said he would stay with me and that what it meant was that we were supposed to be together. He was very supportive and so, when he asked me to marry him, I said yes."

"He sounds like a good man."

"He is."

"Were you living in Barton then?"

"Yes, but then we moved here to Cumberland."

"Alright, you and Bill got married, lived here in Cumberland. What about your daughter? Tell me about her."

With a smile, she explained, "Her name is Joanne. She is eleven years old and in the sixth grade here at St. Patrick's."

"Does she like school?"

"Yes, very much. She especially likes religion when the priests come to talk with them. She says they often get her and the other kids to smile."

"What about your family?"

"My family?"

"Yeah, tell me about your family."

"My mother died when I was twelve. And then my father married a widow who had three children."

"And how many children were in your family?"

"I have two brothers and two sisters."

"So then there were eight kids."

"Eight, that's right. And my father was always working."

"Where did he work?"

"He worked in the mines. He was some kind of boss. Not a big boss, just a boss who made a little more money and did not get as dirty as the others."

"How was it having a stepmother? Did you get along with her?"

"Not very well. Dad was very strict with his kids, especially with us girls. His wife pretty much stayed away from us. He was so strict with us girls that we were hardly ever allowed out."

"How did you and Bill meet?"

"We met at a dance. In fact, I was not allowed to go to the dance that night and so I climbed out of the window."

A smile came over the priest's face.

For years she did not allow herself to consider her act of defiance as funny, but now she did. As she took a moment to enjoy the thought, she stopped talking, causing the priest to look at her.

"Are you okay?" he asked.

"Yes," she said looking back at him. "It's just that I forgot how funny it all was. Me crawling out the window. To go to a dance. It was a wonderful evening. We danced every dance. I did not want the evening to end…" Her voice trailed as she became self conscious that her voice was light and airy.

"Good," added the priest, "it's good to see the humor in things, especially very serious things. So, it sounds as if you have had some tough times."

"What do you mean?"

"Your mother dying when you were still a girl, having to live with your father's new wife and her children. A very strict father."

"Yeah, you know I never really thought of it as hard, only as the way it was."

To hear him say that her life was, indeed, tough was important for her. No one had ever told her that her life had reason to be difficult.

He made her feel at ease by acknowledging her difficulty and helping her discover the humor in her life. Too many around her did not see or help her see any humor in life.

They talked for almost an hour. She explained that Bill and she had drifted apart. What she thought might come to be better, only stayed the same. It moved from moments of deep feeling and connection and communication to an existence that was marked by dinners with few words exchanged. They were seldom alone. And then when she would come to bed, he would be asleep.

She wanted more.

She wanted to go dancing like they had done that first night and would often do before the birth of their daughter. And now, now she could not remember the last time they even went out.

"I no longer hear the music I once heard, like that night at the dance," she said. "The only sound in our life now is the sound of a slow beating drum, which does not even beat all the time."

Father Frank clearly saw that Eileen was disappointed and very much frustrated.

"Well," Father Frank tried to explain, "better or worse is something which we really don't know about. It's different for each couple. The most important person to remember is your daughter. So, try to make time to go out, out on a date like you once did. Bring back the music."

"I know, Father, and I guess that's why I came to see you hoping that maybe talking about it would help."

"Has it?"

"Has it what?"

"Helped?"

"Yes, yes Father, it has helped," she said, glancing at the clock on his desk. "Oh, look at the time. I have to go. I didn't mean to go on like this." She stood and looked about for her coat.

"Please call me in a month to let me know how things are with you and Bill. If necessary, we can set another appointment," he said. "Let me get your coat."

Father Frank walked to the coat rack, lifting and again noticing the fragrance rising from her coat.

"I'll walk you to your car."

"You don't have to do that. Actually I walked."

"You walked here tonight?"

"Yes, it's not that far. I live only a few blocks away."

"Well you are not going to walk home. I will go and get my car and drive you home," he said, opening the door. The two walked the few steps to the front door and as he reached in front of her to open it, he brushed up against her and the two were still for an instant before stepping out onto the porch. It was a long porch and the night was cold, yet there was warmth between them.

"You wait here. I'll be right back."

As he stepped away a train whistle blew.

"Listen, where do you think it's going?" she asked, catching herself as she realized her hand was touching his sleeve. "To Chicago, California?" she asked.

"Probably Pittsburgh with a load of coal," he said, then he looked at her. The slight light from the nearby post in the rectory yard was enough to see into her eyes. There was brightness to them, in which he could almost see the distant place she was looking for.

"You've quite an imagination," he observed.

"Yeah, it comes from being one of eight kids in Barton, Maryland."

He smiled, "You wait here. I'll be right back."

Inside the rectory, he took two steps at a time up to his room. He clicked on the light and from his dresser, picked up a fresh pack of Camels, and remembered his car keys were on the hook in the kitchen. Having changed his suit coat for his favorite grey sweater, he was down the steps and gliding through the hall and into the kitchen, when Father O'Toole, turning from the refrigerator, a bucket of ice in his hand, looked at Frank, who was humming to himself.

"Frank, where have you been? Lynch keeps asking what time your appointment was. How long was it supposed to be?"

"I know, I know. Have you seen my keys? Tell him I'll be there in twenty minutes. I have to go out for cigarettes," he explained, pulling his keys off the hook and making his way out the back door in a manner befitting Fred Astaire.

"One, two, three," he said to himself as he took the steps up to where his car was parked.

He pulled his shiny Buick around the corner and noticed she had moved to the curb at the edge of the sidewalk in the front of the church and was looking at the church in the light of the moon.

"Need a lift?" he said, pulling up alongside of her.

She smiled. He stopped and jumped out of the car and accompanied her around to the passenger side to open the door. Assured her coat was inside, he closed the door and walked around the front of the car through the headlights.

He's nice. He's very nice, she thought to herself as she watched him through the lights.

Inside the car, she hardly noticed the night chill that rushed in with him as he closed his door.

"Where to?"

"I live just past the firehouse. If you take me to the firehouse. I can walk from there."

"Nonsense, I'll take you to your door," he said with an air of insistence.

"Really, that won't be necessary."

By then they were on their way down the street. He reached into his pocket and with one hand on the steering wheel, pulled his cigarettes.

"Would you like a cigarette?" he asked as he took one out of the pack.

Feeling safe in the darkness of the car and having been yearning for one for some time, she accepted. He handed her the one already out and took out another, putting it into his mouth. He lifted his Zippo in a much practiced motion, flicked the metal lid and struck the rough edged wheel against the flint. The cotton wick lit, he reached the flame across in search of the tip of her unlit cigarette.

She took his hand. It was warm and comfortable. She pulled it to the tip of her cigarette and drew in a breath, a deep, cleansing breath, and exhaled. His hand lingered near hers. She thanked him and sat back, feeling a warm glow wash over her.

THE CARD GAME

Frank moved slowly through the rectory kitchen. He opened the ice box and looked at the bottles of beer.

"I think I'll have something a little stronger," he said to himself.

Up the back stairs he counted the steps to himself—"one, two, three." Once at the top, he sighed, opened the door, and surveyed the room and the table. The Monsignor barely looked up from the cards he was holding almost in his face, more to accommodate his nearsightedness than to shield them from the others.

"There you are. Thought you got lost," was Monsignor's welcome, and the opening volley.

"Sorry, Monsignor, I needed cigarettes," he explained trying to lighten the mood, which had become more subdued upon his entrance. "Can't play poker without cigarettes."

"Well, sit here," said the Monsignor, pointing to the chair to his immediate left.

Frank stood at the table with the ice and bottles. He reached for the Jack Daniels, covered three ice cubes in the bottom of the tumbler, and kept pouring until the clear brown liquid was almost to the top.

"Hard day, Frank?" observed the Monsignor.

"No, just long, and it looks like I have some catching up to do," he noticed the almost drained glasses at each of the places of the four card players. Here, on a Friday night, these men of the cloth were all in sport shirts, except Frank who still had his Roman collar on. They could have easily been mistaken for a group of business men.

As Frank sat down he noticed that the Monsignor had more chips than the others. This was not unusual. Most of the time he won.

Frank pulled the chair far enough away from the table to seat himself. Sitting, he pulled his pack of cigarettes out of his pocket, removed one, lit it with his lighter, and placed the silver Zippo on top of the pack almost before the flame was out.

"I'll have five dollars worth of chips," he said, looking to Monsignor to oblige his request.

"Not staying long?" Monsignor asked as he passed the chips over to him.

"May be all I need. Just going to prime the pump," he replied and they were off to their usual sparring.

He pulled his chair a little closer, sipped his Jack Daniels, took a long deep drag of his cigarette, and tried to think about where he was, rather than where he wanted to be. From the other end of the table Father Connor began dealing the cards. Father Joseph Connor was Monsignor's closest friend and the Pastor at St. Mary's, one of the two other Roman Catholic Churches in Cumberland. Connor was ordained with the Monsignor and they stayed close through the years, even though his Roman education and some personal experiences caused him to think a little more than the Monsignor thought priests should.

"What's the game?" Monsignor wanted to know.

"Something I learned in Rome," Father Connor replied.

"You learned something in Rome?" shot Frank.

There were smiles from around the table, even from Monsignor.

"Actually, I learned a lot," he smiled while dealing one card to each player around the table. "But this is a card game."

"Seven card stud. Threes and sevens are wild," he stopped to explain the specifics of this game, "and if the King of Hearts shows up, Kings and whatever card follows are wild and the other wild cards, the threes and sevens, are null and void."

"Why's that?" Father O'Toole wanted to know.

"The King of Hearts is the Pope. And he is infallible. So whatever he says goes."

A subdued chuckle followed as they tried to make some sense of it all while Connor continued to deal.

"How was your appointment, Frank?" asked the Monsignor, bringing the cards up to where he could see them clearly.

"Fine," answered Frank, hoping that would be all.

There were rules, unwritten though they might be, about asking one another about appointments. Then there were the Monsignor's rules, which basically allowed him to pick and choose which of the rules he would keep.

"Was it a woman with a marriage problem?" Monsignor asked while looking intently at his cards. Father Frank pretended that the game distracted him from hearing the question. The Monsignor asked again, "It was a married woman with a problem you had the appointment with tonight, Father?"

Frank, not looking up from his cards, replied, "Yes, it was another married woman with a problem. You know that is my specialty."

Detecting the agitation in Frank's voice, Monsignor moved to one of the others. "Father O'Toole." The Pastor looked at O'Toole who was looking at Frank, trying to figure out what he was thinking about. "Father O'Toole," the older priest pressed on, "do you have the early Mass tomorrow?"

"Yes, Monsignor, I do."

"Would you please remember my niece? My sister called today to tell me that she is involved with a married man. And, well, she asked me to pray for her," he said, glancing at Frank to see his reaction.

"Sure, Monsignor," replied Father O'Toole. "What's her name?"

"Ellen," he replied, causing Frank to look over at him.

"That must be hard," said Frank looking at the Monsignor, "having a niece involved with a married man. How did your sister find out?"

"A friend of the family saw them going into a bar in Pittsburgh," explained Monsignor. "Not once but several times over the course of several weeks. It seemed Thursday was their day to get together."

"Pittsburgh's a big city." observed Frank, "That was quite a coincidence."

"Yes, it was."

"Oh, and there is the Pope," commented Father Connor dealing the next card up to himself.

"And what does this mean?" asked Father Wise, who was staring at the seven and three face up next to a Queen in front of him.

"Well let's see what the next card is. That'll be wild with the three and sevens null and void." He turned the card. "The two of clubs."

Father Wise puffed on his pipe, once, then twice, as if to signal his scorn at this recent turn of events.

Gazing around at the cards, Father Connor commented on the state of things at the present moment.

"Father Wise had three Queens. Father Frank, maybe you have something we can't see," which caused Monsignor to chuckle. "Well, wouldn't that be a surprise."

Father O'Toole had already turned over his cards and was on his way to the bar table.

"Father Wise. Well Father, you may want to just give us some more of your money," said Father Connor turning over two aces and pulling the pile of chips in his direction.

Monsignor wanted him to know his thoughts on the game. "Well, that's a good way to lose money. I thought these Kings and my three would have been enough."

"That's Rome for you," Frank observed. "Always a surprise just when you think you're getting ahead."

"That's it for me," said Father O'Toole, returning to the table and pushing his remaining chips in the direction of the Monsignor. "I have early Mass tomorrow. Cash me out."

"It's not that early," the Pastor responded.

"It is when you've been up since five this morning," Father O'Toole added.

"Five?"

"Yeah, I had to go to the hospital and administer last rites to Mr. Alexander."

"How many times were you at the hospital this week?"

"Two, no, three times. I was there on Monday, again on Wednesday morning and this morning. He stood and put his chair under the table and he began to move away, looking over at Frank, who had been staring at him as he talked about the hospital.

Getting up from the table, Frank asked, "Would anyone like a drink?"

"I would," said Father Connor handing him his glass.

"How about you, Father Wise, Father O'Toole?" Then reluctantly, "How about you Monsignor?"

"Yes, Frank, now that you've asked, the usual."

"Scotch and soda, right?"

"Yes, with only three ice cubes."

"Yeah, that is one thing we have in common, only three ice cubes."

As Frank walked over to the table, he turned back, to recap the drink order. "Jack Daniels, Scotch, and, oh yeah, I will have another Jack Daniels," he said, pointing to himself as an attempt at humor. He seemed distracted. The others noticed, but chose not to say anything. As he poured the drinks he was humming to himself.

This was not unusual. He was often concerned about the people he met with and continued to wonder how they were doing long after the meetings. Tonight was different. Tonight he was more distant, more pre-occupied. He was still with her, in some way, as he took another drag on his cigarette and almost poured the soda over the edge of the glass.

Returning to the table, first with Father Connor's drink, then with his own, Monsignor looked up and asked, "And where's mine?"

"Oh, I'm sorry," Father Frank said returning to the bar to pick up the Monsignor's drink. "Here you are."

Seeing that Frank noticed that the cards were already dealt, the Monsignor explained that they were not sure when he was coming back, so they started the next game.

"That's okay," Frank assured them. "I'll just sit and watch how the pros do it."

Looking around the room, Frank pondered whether the other priests had the same experience with people as he did.

Do they wonder about how they are doing? Think about what else might have been said, not said. Do they think people really do what they say, follow their advice? Monsignor always had the right answer and it was not something anyone ever even thought of challenging. Wise, well Wise smokes the pipe and knows Canon Law. O'Toole and I were in seminary together and I know he tries to sympathize with the people he ministers. Connor's face displays the wrinkles, the lines of someone who worries and stays with his parishioners.

Sipping his Jack Daniels, Father Frank found his thoughts drifting from the room to Eileen, wondering what she was doing.

"Are you ready to play?" Monsignor asked.

"Yeah, I'm in," Frank replied, coming back from his dream.

After a few hands, the card game began to wind down and the real game, the game of wits, began.

"Father Connor," Frank began.

"Yes, Frank," Connor said.

"Supposing," Frank continued.

"Not this again," interjected Monsignor.

"Let him go, Bob," Connor quieted Monsignor.

"Supposing a married woman comes to see you," Frank continued. "She's unhappy in her marriage…"

"Why is she coming to see you?" Monsignor interrupted.

Only slightly frustrated, Frank said, again, "She's unhappy in her marriage."

41

"So, why is she coming to see a priest? Our job is not to make people happy," Monsignor Lynch explained.

"I know that. I suppose you have never met with a woman, or for that matter, a man," he paused.

"I can't remember talking with a man about his being unhappy in his marriage," Monsignor quipped.

Frank looked at the Monsignor for only an instant, then turned back to Father Connor. "I just wanted to hear how Father Connor would handle this."

"She says that she's unhappy?" Connor wanted to know.

"What do you mean?" Frank asked, unsure of Father Connor's line of reason.

"Did she tell you she was unhappy?" Connor asked, lifting his glass to take a drink.

"Yes, she told me she was unhappy."

"Well, did she tell you why she was unhappy?" Connor placed his glass next to the ash tray as if it were a gavel and picked up his cigarette. "Because everyone is unhappy at one time or another."

"Well," Frank replied, "she's unhappy because, she says, because there's no love, no feeling between her and her husband."

"You mean no excitement," chuckled Monsignor. "Too many people want excitement."

"Did she tell you why there is no feeling?"

"Well, no. Except that her husband is away a lot."

"How much?"

"He leaves Monday and returns Thursday."

"A salesman?"

"I think."

"Do they have children?"

"One. A girl."

"How old is she?"

"She is almost thirteen."

"Has she thought about leaving?" Connor wanted to know. And, as Frank nonchalantly began to answer, he noticed the look of concern around the room and heard Monsignor Lynch's groan.

"Yes, actually, that is one of the reasons she came to see me," said Frank. "She wanted to know what the church says about that…about leaving."

"And what did you tell her?" Monsignor interrupted.

"That I'd see her in a month," Frank said, smiling behind his cards.

"That's always a safe answer," commented Father O'Toole, who had lingered long enough to be interested in the conversation.

As the attention shifted to whose play it was in the card game, Connor, from behind his cards and in a haze of smoke, asked to no one in particular, "Should people be happy? Do they or we, for that matter, have a right to be happy?"

A thoughtful silence fell over the priests.

"Are we going to play cards or talk?" Monsignor puffed his annoyance.

"Well," Father Wise began, "according to scripture 'eternal happiness' is our reward and is what we are on earth preparing for. It comes after death."

"You have to remember, Father Wise, that it's a story," Father O'Toole weighed in. "The scriptures are stories, stories to try and get the message across."

"And what is the message?" Wise wanted to know.

Monsignor, who was not to be left out of the discussion, quoted from the Gospel of John, "My kingdom is not of this world.' But what does all this have to do with people, a woman

43

actually, wanting to be happy in Cumberland in 1944, while our country is at war?"

"I just asked a question," Connor continued, "and am I supposed to be happy with these answers? Well I'm not and I guess that's okay from what I'm hearing."

"How many cards do you want?" Father Wise asked Father Frank.

"Two. What's wrong with wanting to be happy?" Frank queried the group as he picked up the cards and moved them beside the three in his hand.

"Happiness is fleeting," Father Wise noted. "It's like playing cards. Sometimes you get a good hand, win the pot, and you're happy. Then, anticipating another win, you keep playing with new enthusiasm and you lose and you lose and, just as you are ready to quit, you win another hand and start all over again."

"And while you're losing," Frank wondered, "what are you feeling?"

"I don't know if you're feeling anything," Father O'Toole observed. "You may be still feeling the excitement of the victory. I hadn't thought much about it."

"Are you unhappy?" Wise wanted to know.

"*Un*happy?" Frank asked a little irritated.

"Yeah. You don't look happy," O'Toole said. "You look as if something is weighing on your mind."

"Well, I'm not winning. That doesn't make me happy," Frank said and wanting to keep the conversation going added, "Tell me you are all happy?"

"I try not to think about it," Father Wise commented. "I try to keep busy with my prayers, my duties, appointments, celebrating Mass. Yes, I can say I'm happy when I'm celebrating Mass."

"All the time?" Frank asked.

"What do you mean all the time?" Monsignor Lynch parried.

"When you say Mass on Sundays or during the week?" Frank wanted to know.

"I guess I would have to say more during the week," Wise answered after a slight hesitation.

"Now, for me," Connor began, "celebrating Mass on Sundays is more of a celebration. During the week, it is more private prayer. There are only a few people there and, well, I often feel as if I'm alone."

"That's what I like about weekday Mass. I feel as if I am alone, alone with God," Wise explained.

"What about the people?" Frank asked.

"Yeah, what about the people?" Connor joined Frank.

"Well they're there," Wise continued.

"And?" Frank interrupted.

"Well, when I say Mass," Wise went on, "I am celebrating the Eucharist with and for the glory of God."

"And the people."

"They are there watching me. Most are praying silently," Wise said, suggesting that, isn't that the way it was supposed to be.

"Well, at least you're happy," Frank wryly observed.

"I guess it's up to me," commented Monsignor Lynch.

Frank wanted Monsignor to weigh in on the subject. He asked, "And what makes *you* happy?"

"Winning," replied Monsignor while sliding his chips across the table. "I raise you fifty cents."

"I'm not surprised," commented Connor.

"Is that all that makes you happy?" Frank wanted to know.

"Actually, besides winning, I like to go fishing." Observed Monsignor.

"For souls?" Frank joked, looking for at least a smile from the table.

"Funny, I hadn't thought about that in a while," Monsignor Lynch said smiling. "I meant fishing for fish, taking a chance, sort of like this game."

Monsignor looked around the table.

"In the early morning," he began, "when I am up at Deep Creek Lake, the fog begins to lift, the water laps at the boat as I turn off the outboard motor. The interrupted quiet returns. A stillness comes over the lake. The ripples I created when leaving the dock settle and the water's surface returns to a glass-like sheen." His words softened with each syllable.

Frank looked at Monsignor Lynch as if seeing him for the first time. He sensed a peacefulness, an ease in his usually scowling face, tranquil, like the lake water he just described.

"When was the last time you were up at the lake?" Connor asked.

Thinking for a second, Monsignor said, "Late April, early May was the last time I was up there. You know, I don't remember if I caught any fish. I only remember being out there on the lake and the quiet and the stillness."

"What about you other guys?" Connor asked, leaving Monsignor Lynch to his thoughts. "What makes you happy?"

"A good smoke and a book," puffed Wise.

"And you, Father O'Toole?" Connor rounding out the group, "What makes you happy?"

Father O'Toole paused and looked more into the room than at anyone, "Getting into my prayers."

Frank squinted, surmising that O'Toole's response was what he thought a priest should say, what the Monsignor wanted to hear him say, more than what he actually believed.

"Getting into your prayers?" Frank asked a little exasperated. "I don't know what that means."

"You probably wouldn't," observed Father Wise. "It has to do with what it means to be a priest, paying attention to what's important. Like saying the office every day at the appointed time."

"Are you saying I don't say the office?" Frank shot back even more exasperated, but in defense of what exactly he was not quite sure.

"No, I didn't say that," assured Father Wise.

"Well, what did you say?" asked Frank.

"I said...," but before he could continue, Monsignor interrupted.

"Are we going to play cards or gab?"

"Gab?" Father Wise looking puzzled. "What is gab?"

"I think it's a Pittsburgh word that made its way down the road," Connor helped explain. "It means to talk, more like mindless chatter, words in search of sentences, complete thoughts, you know."

"Well, talking about one's happiness is not really mindless, now is it?" Father Wise said.

"Happiness," Frank looked at the hand that had been dealt him, "is certainly not in these cards. I guess for me a good book, a fine meal with friends, a walk on the city streets or, in the country, just being outside...."

"What about priestly things?" Monsignor saw an opening.

"Isn't the Bible a good book?" Frank replied. "And, as I understand it, the Mass is a celebration commemorating the Last Supper, a meal where Jesus was gathered with his closest friends."

Father O'Toole spoke up, "Yeah, some friends. Where did they go during his walk after supper?"

"How many cards?" Connor tried to divert attention back to the game.

"I'm okay," said Monsignor.

"Frank?"

"Can I get five?" said Frank with a smile. "Okay, I'll take two."

"Okay. What have you all got?" Monsignor wanted to move the game along.

"You mean have, don't you Monsignor?" Frank said, correcting the elder's grammar.

"Whatever. Have. Got," Monsignor said. "I have got to see what is in your hands so that I can collect my money."

Three of the priests slid their cards into the center, but Frank hesitated and then fanned his cards out on the table. He declared, "A royal straight flush."

"Damn," Monsignor exhaled as he slid his cards face down into the pile.

As Frank reached to pull the pile of chips to him, Monsignor Lynch stared at him with the familiar look that conveyed the sentiment, "Who do you think you are?"

"One more hand for me," said Father Wise. "I'm bushed."

"Okay with me," said one then another.

"How about that Pope game?" asked O'Toole.

"Not that mumbo jumbo," Monsignor replied.

"What mumbo jumbo?" Frank wanted to know. "The game, or infallibility?"

"Probably both. How many of our parishioners can even spell it, let alone understand what it means?"

"Isn't that our job to help them understand it?" O'Toole asked.

"Sure, sure Father, that's our job to take the irrelevant and make it relevant," Frank said with more than a touch of sarcasm.

"Enough with the silliness," Monsignor wanted to move on.

"Silliness?" Connor queried. "You think our work is silly?"

"Well," Monsignor paused until he was sure he had Frank's attention, "silly? No. Questionable? Yes. It seems we're always telling people what to do and how to live."

"Usually in answer to questions," Connor added, "and not all the time. And hopefully, with some conversation, some context within which we explain the options."

"What options?" Wise wanted to know.

"The options, the choices that people have," Connor said.

"Options? Choices? What are you talking about?" Monsignor asked.

"Conscience. Don't you all tell people about conscience?" Connor asked, puzzled.

"Oh, you mean that conscience is the supreme dictate of will?" O'Toole asked.

"Yes," Connor said, relieved that someone knew what he was talking about.

"I never quite got that," Wise observed.

Lifting his glass and taking a good sip, Connor attempted to explain: "Conscience is the supreme dictate of will and you must follow it, whatever."

"You mean that if people think it's okay to do something, like practice birth control, it's okay?" Wise asked.

"Well, okay may be a little strong. Let's say they must follow their conscience," Connor clarified.

"You know," Wise muttered, "sometimes I don't understand our Church."

"Sometimes?" Monsignor Lynch added.

"What do you mean?" Frank asked. "What's to understand? The people know what their expectations are: Pay, Pray, and Obey. That's not too complicated."

"Yeah, but what about this conscience thing? How many people even know about it?" O'Toole asked.

"What's there to know?" asked Wise. "Do we have to tell everyone, everything?"

"Well, isn't that a little deceptive?" Frank asked.

"Why do you think it's deceptive?" Connor asked.

"It's not telling everything," Frank pointed out.

"Does a mother tell a child everything she knows?" Connor asked.

"Well, no," Frank acknowledged.

There was silence.

Then Connor—in a soft, demonstrative voice—said, "Remember the Church is your mother."

"Yeah, and sometimes your mother is not always truthful." Frank pointed out.

"The Church is your mother," stated Connor, "and sometimes she lies to you… to protect you. Your mother is a sinner…but nonetheless, still your mother." Connor's comment silenced the room again. He looked at his fellow priests and said, "When you can love your mother as she is, not as you think she is, then you have faith."

"Sometimes, you go beyond me," said Monsignor putting his cards on the table. "I'm going to bed."

"What's wrong Monsignor?" asked Connor. "Did I offend you?"

"No, maybe just helped me see something I have not been able to see," Monsignor Lynch said as he stood. "Something I didn't want to hear, but knew, something I need to think about."

The rest of the group stayed for one more hand. It was almost Saturday morning. It was the beginning of the weekend, their busy days.

THE MOVIE

Had it been three months since that Friday night when they had their first appointment? Eileen asked herself as she listened to the phone ring there in St. Patrick's rectory.

"Hello. This is Saint Patrick's parish office," said the voice on the other end of the line. It was the parish secretary.

"May I speak with Father McGowan?" Eileen asked.

"Father McGowan is in a meeting," explained the secretary. "Would you like to leave a message?"

She paused, "Yes, please."

"What is your name?"

"My name is..." she hesitated again. "My name is Eileen Hamilton. I am calling to set an appointment to see him."

"Does he have your phone number?" the secretary asked.

"I don't know," she answered.

"Well, why don't you give it to me, just in case."

"Columbia 1-4648." she said.

"I will give him the message."

"Thank you," she said and hung up the receiver.

Eileen sat looking at the phone wondering if giving out the phone number was the right thing to do. *What if he calls and Bill answers?* she thought. *Maybe he'll call as soon as he gets out of the meeting.*

She stood and went into the kitchen to fix herself a cup of coffee. She sat at the white metal topped table stirring the second spoonful of sugar into the cup of steaming hot coffee as if she were stirring a magic potion. She pulled a cigarette from the pack that was always next to the ever present cup of coffee. She lit it and, as she exhaled, remembered his hand lighting her cigarette that night.

On the radio "Begin the Beguine" played. She reached over, turned up the volume, and, as she so often did, allowed herself to drift to another place as she inhaled the smoke… *There, on a spring day, she and the priest sat quietly and talked of the day as a waiter poured each a glass of wine.*

The ringing phone pulled her back and she moved to the next room to answer it.

"Hello," she said anxiously, anticipating the voice would be his.

"Hello? Hello, Eileen, is that you?" the voice on the other end asked, not recognizing her light, almost airy voice.

"Yes, this is Eileen," she replied, realizing the voice was not the one she had hoped for.

"It's Bill," said her husband.

"Oh, hi Bill. Something wrong?" she asked because he seldom called during the day.

"No, nothing's wrong," he said as his words slowed. "I called because I know we're supposed to go out this evening."

"Yeah. I have a babysitter for Joanne. She is going to Mary's to spend the night."

"I'm sorry, Eileen," Bill explained. "I just found out I have to drive to Pittsburgh for a meeting."

Eileen was not sure if the news disappointed or relieved her. She felt a certain relief at not having to face the possibility that their night together would not have worked out well. She sighed and assured him, "Don't worry. We can do it another time. What time do you have to leave?"

"By noon." Bill said. "Can you pack me a change of clothes and a couple packs of cigarettes? I'll be there by around 11:30."

"Okay," she responded dutifully.

"Thanks. See you then," he finished and hung up the phone.

Walking through the living room to their bedroom she tried to remember if she had gone to the drycleaners to pick-up his "Pittsburgh" suit as he liked to call it.

She went to the closet and saw that it was not there. *I'll have to walk to the drycleaners...what time is it?* she asked herself, looking for the clock on the counter.

"10:30." she said aloud, "I have enough time." She walked into the kitchen to the drawer where she kept the money and the cleaner slips.

Shuffling through the drawer, she found the cleaner receipt and counted five one-dollar bills and noted, "I better pick up a carton of cigarettes."

She snuffed out her cigarette in the ashtray on the table. She put her coffee cup in the sink. Reaching the front door she stared at the coats on the rack and tried to decide which of her two coats to wear. Taking a coat with one arm, she opened the door. Surprised that, although it was winter, it was warmer than she expected, she wondered if she even needed a coat. She decided to wear it as she looked down at her well-worn dress and pulled her simple black coat around herself.

The street was quiet. She did not know any of the few people she passed, but still she offered each of them a smile. Approaching the cleaners, she saw her sister Mary coming out. The two smiled and asked how each other was and Mary began, "We're going to have French fries and fish, and after dinner the girls are going to bake a chocolate cake."

"Bill has to go to Pittsburgh this afternoon," Eileen interrupted, "some business meeting."

"Does that mean that Joanne won't be coming over?" Mary asked.

"Well...," Eileen began, then paused as she remembered Bill's suit, "let me get Bill's suit before I forget."

Eileen stepped back onto the sidewalk next to her waiting sister.

"Listen, Eileen. The girls are expecting Joanne and I'm sure she is looking forward to coming. Why not let her come. It will give you an evening to yourself."

Hesitating, Eileen pulled her coat a little closer around her.

"Well...I guess, I don't want to disappoint Joanne." Eileen said with a sense of resignation. "Okay. What time do you want her there?"

"We eat at six," Mary said, "so, can you have her there by 5:30?"

"Sure. I'll have her there by 5:30," Eileen smiled at the possibility of some time on her hands. "Thanks."

"So, this cancelled date," Mary began. "Things are going better?"

"Well, not really," Eileen said as the two walked down the street.

Eileen dared not to mention that the idea had come from her conversation with a priest. God forbid any of them would have to go to see a priest about their marriage.

"Bill goes to work, comes home," Eileen said. "I fix his meals, clean his clothes, cook and clean and..."

"And what's so bad about that?" Mary wanted to know.

"I guess it's okay." Eileen tried to convince herself as the two walked amidst the other Friday afternoon errand runners. "I want more. I thought we could travel, but the only traveling is when Bill goes to Pittsburgh on business."

"Can you go with him?" Mary asked.

"What would I do? Bill will be in meetings and we don't have any extra money for shopping," Eileen said listing her reasons for not even thinking about going with Bill. "And, besides, Bill and I really don't do well together, alone. We seem to be in different worlds."

As the two approached the street where each would go her separate way, Mary noticed that Eileen was staring off into the distance, just like she would when they were young girls in Barton. She stared out into the clouds that almost touched the mountains that created the valley they lived in. Mary often had to shake Eileen back into present reality.

"Eileen, Eileen," Mary said, again trying to bring her sister back from wherever she had drifted. "Are you alright?"

"Oh, yeah. I'm fine," Eileen said.

As the two parted, Mary reminded Eileen to have Joanne at her house by 5:30 and wished her sister well, hugged her and kissed her on the cheek, telling her to be sure to enjoy her evening, her time alone.

Back at the house, Eileen hung the suit on the door in the bedroom. In a somewhat practiced motion she removed two shirts, underwear and socks from the dresser. She then went to the closet to find the suitcase. She placed the suitcase on the bed for

Bill to pack. Returning to the kitchen, she noticed it was almost 11:30, and as she reached for a cigarette, she remembered that she had forgotten to stop to pick up a carton. She looked in the drawer and saw there were still four packs in her carton. *He'll just have to smoke Old Golds today*, she said to herself, lifting two packs from the carton and placing them on the kitchen table. Sitting there she turned on the radio and waited. She was in the middle of a song and a cigarette when Bill arrived and quickly went to the bedroom to pack with only a word of apology for not keeping their date, and promising to make it up to her. He returned, suitcase in hand. He asked her to tell Joanne he loved her and tell her that he would bring her a souvenir from Pittsburgh. As Eileen sat acknowledging his words, she remained lost in the haze of her cigarette and the music on the radio. He asked if there were cigarettes. Eileen handed him two packs of Old Golds.

"I forgot to get your cigarettes," she said in response to his not-so-pleased look. He gave her a peck on the cheek and the obligatory, "Love you." Then he was gone.

With Joanne cared for, Eileen pondered getting dressed and going to the movies. The idea of going to the movies alone on a Friday night was as much an invitation as it was a challenge.

She found a seat in the last row at the end of the aisle so that she could slip out as soon as the movie's credits rolled. Sitting there, she felt alone and wondered about him, the priest. Why had he not returned her call?

She inspected the ornate theater. She remembered coming here to see movies with Bill on their early dates. This had long been a place to come and see live entertainment. It was always a

refuge for escape seekers who lived in Cumberland, but longed
to be somewhere else. She sat there alone, ate her popcorn, and
watched newsreels of the war some thought would never end.
Listening to a clear, reassuring voice talk as if the war was coming
to an end, she wiped a tear from her eye as she viewed images
of bodies of men on some beach on an island somewhere in the
Pacific.

A tap on her shoulder brought her back to the theater.

"Eileen," came a voice she knew but could almost not believe
was real. Father Frank pointed to the seat next to her. " Is anyone
sitting there?" he asked.

"Well, no, I don't think so," she stammered as she looked up,
as much in disbelief as pleased to see Father Frank standing in the
aisle next to her.

"May I sit down?" he asked.

Not sure what to say, she paused, "Sure, I guess."

"Do you come to the movies often?" he asked as he passed her
and settled into the seat next to her.

"Yes," she replied, not sure what else to say.

"Me, too," he said. "I find them a great way to get away from it
all, to relax."

She could not believe it was really him. The two of them at the
movies, on a Friday night.

The Warner Brothers logo faded out as the name of the film
faded in. Eileen read the words aloud, "To Have and Have Not."

"Interesting title," remarked the priest.

The name HUMPHREY BOGART flashed on the screen and
she smiled to herself. "Isn't he the guy that was in Casablanca?" she
asked.

"Yeah, that's him," he whispered back.

"Hey, did you see that?"

"What?" she wondered because the movie had not yet started.

"William Faulkner was one of the writers who worked on this screenplay," he whispered leaning a little closer this time. "I wonder what Hemingway thought about that?"

"Who's Hemingway?" she asked.

"He wrote the book the movie is based on," whispered Father Frank.

"Oh," she replied, feeling a bit uninformed.

The movie was set in Martinique, a far away island that fueled Eileen's imagination, which in turn swept her away from lonely isolated Cumberland. Books did not do the trick for her; movies were her ticket. She came at least once a week, usually on Wednesday. Wednesday afternoons were difficult for her. Joanne was at school and Bill at work. And she was at home, alone with her chores and her thoughts. By noon she had finished the cleaning and had been to the grocery store. Often she would find herself sitting at the kitchen table, listening to the radio, smoking a cigarette and day dreaming. She would move her foot to the music and hum or sing the words softly to herself imagining herself anywhere but where she was, nowhere. To break the monotony, she went to the movies, alone. So, as she settled in this evening, she felt a bit awkward having company, especially a priest.

It was a time of war. It was a time when most everyone was involved in the efforts to defeat one of the world's evils. Whether the oppression came in the form of Nazi Fascism or Japanese Imperialism, most everyone in small towns across America was trying to defeat the evil so that the world could be safe and free. While her oppression was not of such magnitude, Eileen also struggled to be free. She was still young and attractive, but living in a place where she could not be free to do what she wanted.

The mountains that embraced Cumberland, mountains that many found comfortable, served as a prison to her.

At the movies, she was at ease if even for just a few hours. But tonight, she was in a different place, perplexed with feelings that were becoming more complex than the plot that unfurled on the screen. She liked that there was a man sitting next to her. She liked that she could inhale his aftershave, the scent of a man clean shaven and fresh, something she had enjoyed but not for some time. That this man at her side was a man with whom she had shared some of her struggle, stirred in her some inner part that had not been touched for some time, perhaps not ever. She noticed his hand on the armrest and remembered how soft and firm it was that night he reached across to light her cigarette. She looked up to the screen to keep herself from reaching out to touch his hand.

"Am I blue," sang Hoagy Carmichael catching her attention. "You'd be too if each plan with your maiden fell through."

The story on the screen did not appeal to her as much as the story that began to take shape in her head. As Bogart and Bacall moved together through the story, Eileen felt herself moving closer and closer to the man at her side.

"You know how to whistle?" Lauren Bacall softly said to Bogart. "Just put your lips together and blow."

Eileen caught herself puckering her lips and thought she heard more than a few soft whistling sounds from among the others around her.

As the credits began to roll he watched.

"Well," he said, turning his head in her direction, "what do you think?"

"About what?" Eileen asked.

"The movie. Did you like the movie?" he asked again, noticing that Eileen was half out of her seat, as was her habit to rush out before the lights came on and someone might see her, alone, at the movies. He asked his next question before she answered the first one, "Where are you going?"

"I have to go," she said standing, and making her way up the aisle with her coat in her arms.

He sat for a second more, glanced at the credits before getting up to see if he could catch up with her.

Outside as the audience made their way into the street, he looked right, then left, noticing that she was moving down the street. He almost had to run to catch up to her, hoping to reach her before she got too far away.

"Boy, you're quite a walker," he said as he caught up with her.

"Oh, hello," she said with half a smile. "You're pretty fast yourself."

The two walked for two or three more blocks before he asked, "Where are you going in such a hurry?"

"Home," she said not so certain that she really wanted to be saying the words.

"What about a drink?" he asked.

A drink, she thought to herself, sounded wonderful and, at the same time, more than a bit incongruous. *Here's a priest asking me, a married woman, to go out for a drink in Cumberland, Maryland. Half the people in Cumberland probably heard him ask me.*

With a smile on her lips, she asked, "And where could we get a drink in this town without everyone noticing?"

"If you want the drink, I know where we can go," he explained trying to assure her that this could happen.

"Okay, sure," she said with more than a little interest as to where this would happen. "I'll have a drink with you. But only one"

THE KISS

She was surprised when they pulled into the parking lot of the rectory.

"Are you...," she started.

"Don't worry," he interrupted, anticipating her question. "No one is here."

Inside, he escorted her to the parlor that was actually next to the room where they met the first time. Closing the door, he directed her to a couch and asked what she would like to drink.

"Well, what do you have?" she asked.

"This is a rectory," he replied. "What do you want?"

"I don't know. I don't drink much. Once I had a drink that had vodka and, I think it was something like grapefruit juice. But I don't know what it was, but it was good."

"Oh, well now that would be a Tom Collins to the rest of the world," he said smiling.

"Oh," she said, "is that what goes into a Tom Collins?"

"I'll be right back," he said starting to leave the room. "Would you like a cigarette?" He said stepping closer and pulling the pack from his pocket. It was as if he had read her mind.

"Yes," she said aloud, while thinking to herself, *I'm dying for a cigarette.*

Half tilting the pack in her direction, she smiled and, restraining her eagerness nodded a "thank you." Before she could reach to take a cigarette from the pack he removed two and put both in his mouth. He dragged the flame to the tips of the cigarettes, carefully removed one and handed it to her. Her fingers reached out to receive the cigarette. She thanked him and moved the white papered cylinder to her mouth. As she seated herself, she took a long, slow drag of the cigarette. He paused before he stepped to the door to get their drinks.

"Here, let me turn on some music to keep you company." He walked over and turned on the radio that sat on the shelf next to the window.

There in the room with the light of a single lamp and the glow of the cigarette and its thin stream of smoke, she sat listening to music that she usually listened to alone while dreaming of just such a moment, a moment that was now surreal. She smiled as she listened to the words of "Sentimental Journey" swim through her head, "Seven. That's the time we leave for heaven...."

She thought he had been gone a long time. She began to wonder if he was coming back, worried that someone else might open the door.

"Here you go," came his voice as he closed the door behind him. "One Tom Collins."

He handed her the drink. He paused and looked at the radio. "Begin the Beguine." he said, " Do you like this?"

"Yes," she said, "I like all kinds of music."

"Soothes the soul," he added.

"Oh," she said accepting his explanation. "Is that what this is?"

"What?" he queried.

"My soul being soothed," she answered.

Realizing she was responding to his comment, he laughed slightly.

"What am I doing?" she asked as if she had become aware of where she was.

"You are having a drink," he explained.

"Yes, but where and with who?" she pretended to be looking for an answer.

"With your new friend," he quipped.

"Oh, is that what you are? A new friend?" her eyes moved to his.

"Well, I would hope we can be friends," he said.

Taking a large sip of her drink, "This is very good."

"You don't have to drink it all at once," he said cautioning her.

"I didn't realize how thirsty I was. I had eaten a bag of popcorn at the movie before you got there," she explained.

The drink increased her bravado, and she felt an excitement rise up within her, but she also felt a tinge of discomfort.

"What time is it?" she asked.

"Still early," he said without looking at his watch.

"And what time is still early?" she followed, trying to get a more specific answer.

"10:30." He said glancing at the clock on the mantle across the room.

"I better be going soon," she said snuffing her cigarette and taking another sip of her drink.

"What's the hurry?" he asked.

Then she remembered there actually was no hurry. Bill was in Pittsburgh and Joanne out for the night.

"I guess I can stay a little while longer. Where are the others?" she asked.

"What others?" he replied.

"The others who live here," she asked almost quizzically.

"Oh, them. They are up at the Forty Hours at St. Peter's in Westernport," he explained.

"Forty Hours?" she asked.

"Whenever one of the parishes has Forty Hours it is an occasion for all the priests to get together for dinner and it usually goes on late into the night," he explained.

"And what about you?" she inquired.

"Me?" he asked.

"Yeah, you," she pressed. "Why didn't you go?"

"Well, as someone once observed about me and my fellow priests," he said moving closer, "I don't always seem to do well in that company for long periods of time."

She sat still as he moved a bit closer.

"So, what did you like best about the movie?" he asked.

"That it was on an island, far away from here." She said staring out into the room as if at the island.

"You really don't like it here, do you?" he observed.

"Well, it's not that I don't like it here. It's just that I would like to see other places," her eyes glistened as she talked. "Here, I feel trapped. I want to see the rest of the world."

She finished her drink and set the glass on the small table in front of her.

"I want to go to New York and see a play." She stood and paced as if crossing a stage. "I wonder what it would be like to go to California where it doesn't snow all winter, or even Florida. I have been here all my life. Sometimes I feel bad that I feel bad about being here. Yet, there is something about wanting more. I don't know if I told you that my family is descended from pioneers. We came up here from, I can never remember, either Virginia or some place near Baltimore. And so, maybe it's just in my blood."

He sat and watched as she excitedly described walking down Broadway on a winter's day amidst all the people and honking taxi horns. She described herself sitting at a bar in Manhattan noticing a famous movie star walk in. After awhile, she paused.

"Would you like another drink?" he asked.

Reluctantly, after looking again into her empty glass, she accepted his offer, "One more then I have to be going."

He returned and, as he handed her the glass, "Here's your Tom Collins, Miss Eileen."

Now she was seated again and she took it from his hand, and sipped it slowly.

"I am sorry that I went on like that," Eileen said, "but I just get so frustrated sometimes with living here. It's not so much living as surviving. And, I am sorry, but I want more. Can I have another cigarette?"

"You know," as he handed her a cigarette and lighting it, "you are even more attractive when you are on your 'High Horse.'"

"High Horse? What does that mean?" she asked.

"When you are making your ideas known as if you are royalty astride your mount proclaiming...well, proclaiming whatever," he replied.

Moving a bit closer, he whispered, "I find you very attractive."

The silence was palpable. She turned her head down and just a bit away. As she began to turn back toward him, he had moved even closer. His arm was around her shoulder reaching out to comfort her as her head began to turn to him. He had moved close enough that his breath was warm on her cheek and, as she continued to lift her head, he inhaled her fragrance mixed with the smell of grapefruit and the hint of alcohol.

The kiss was soft. He had leaned over as she moved her head in his direction. Their lips touched.

Her hand moved to his face. She was torn between pushing it away and pulling it closer.

Their faces separated slightly.

"I wish I could say I was sorry, but I…," he began but before he could say another word she had touched her index finger to his lips.

They kissed. Their breathing came together as if each was not complete without the other. They kissed as if this kiss, like all first kisses, was the beginning of something mysterious. They rediscovered the joy of touching another human in such as unique way. It was more than the warmth of the touch; they had found one another and were giving to each other something that neither had known for some time, if ever. They felt safe with each other. They were nurturing one another. They could not seem to stop. They kept going on and on pulling each other closer and closer, until they were lying on the couch, bodies pressed together.

"I better go," she said suddenly attempting to push away, but not really wanting to.

"Please stay," he pleaded.

"No, really. I need to go. I don't know what I am doing here. It's as if I am looking for a way out of here and you, you, who have been other places, may know how, may know the way…," *The way to where?* she wondered. "Will you drive me home?" she asked as she sat up and straightened her dress.

"Sure," he said, pulling himself up to a seated position.

The ride home was quiet. She felt warm and comfortable in an uncomfortable way. At some point, he reached over and took her hand. It was as warm and soft and as comfortable as she remembered.

Once at her place, he pulled to the curb, they smoked another cigarette. And as she pulled away from one last kiss, she looked over at him. She seemed to be half awake and more in a dream. The alcohol gave way to something more, lessening her hesitation, something more as the two made their way through the two rooms to the bedroom, stopping every few steps, not too long, only long enough for another embrace and a kiss until they were on her bed.

As she glanced at the clock next to her bed, she began to realize what she had done. It was three o'clock in the morning and she was in bed with her priest. She felt a mixture of pleasure and angst. She was very still. Then she smiled, and asked herself, "*What shall I call you, you, my priest?*" Then she remembered the name plate on his desk, FR Francis McGowan. "*I will call you FR.*"

SATURDAY MORNING

"Begin the...Begin," Eileen whispered aloud as she awoke.

"I think it's actually Begin the *Beguine*," Frank replied.

"Oh, I'm sorry. I didn't realize I was talking out loud," said Eileen turning over in bed to face the back of Frank, who she thought was still sleeping.

"That's okay. I'm awake," said Frank turning to face her.

The two lay very still facing one another. There was enough light for each of them to see the other.

"Did you sleep?" he asked.

Nodding her head yes she held herself back from moving closer.

"You?" she asked.

"Yes. What time is it?" he asked lifting his wrist so he could see the time.

"7:20," he said in a soft voice, "I must be going."

"Can I make you a cup of coffee?" she asked as she lifted herself up in the bed pulling the sheet around herself.

"That would be nice, but I really must be going," he responded as he turned away from her to sit himself and go about gathering his clothes.

She said nothing. It was all in her head.

Why? Why do you have to go? I really want you to stay. Can't we have coffee? Let's make love again. When will I see you next?

He dressed. She watched, holding her words within.

"Eileen," he began as he walked around the foot of the bed, "I had a wonderful time last night."

Her eyes were fixed on his. She nodded in agreement.

"What happened was…," he began sitting on the bed beside her.

"Don't say a word," she said moving a finger to his lips. "Don't say a word."

She pulled him close. She kissed him gently and said, "I know you have to go. So, go. You know where I will be."

She softly pushed him away from her bed and lay back down. She buried her head in his pillow as she heard the door close. She drifted off to where she could continue the story.

The telephone ring startled her. She started to get out of bed and realized she was naked. She scurried for something to cover herself. Her robe was not on the bed where it usually was, so she pulled the top cover off the bed and wrapped herself in it managing to get to the phone by the fifth ring.

"Hello," she said trying not to sound too exasperated.

"Mommy," came the excited voice.

"Joanne," Eileen said, her voice softening. "How are you? Is everything alright?"

"Mommy. Can I stay here today? Aunt Mary wants to take us to the movies," said Joanne.

"Well, let me talk to Aunt Mary."

Joanne rarely got to go to the movies with her cousins so Eileen and Mary agreed that she would be home for supper. Eileen walked slowly back to her bedroom wrapped in a blanket. She smiled as she felt the slightly quilted fabric against her skin.

"Now what am I going to do?" she asked herself.

Joanne kept her busy and she preferred being busy. Time alone for her was time to think. She usually did not like to think, to think about all she wanted but what little she had. Today was different.

She took a leisurely bath. The water warmed her skin. It reminded her of him. She pulled her cotton robe around her and walked to the kitchen. Sitting at the kitchen table, she drew the flame from the tip of the match to her cigarette. She was back with him that Friday night of their first appointment, feeling his hand as he lit her cigarette.

Eileen wanted to call someone. She wanted to tell everyone about her night at the movie. She wanted to tell everyone about this man who made her feel so right. Then she remembered he was a priest and she was a married woman. For a moment she was back in the darkness that she knew too well, a foreboding feeling that something was wrong. *How could something that felt so right be wrong?* She refused to let anything interfere with this joy she felt.

She decided to walk into town. Given there was no hurry she took her time to find a dress befitting her mood. She spent as much time as she needed putting on her make-up and combing her hair to be sure she looked as good as she felt.

Outside, as she began her walk, she looked up at the sky and the mountains. Their usually looming presence was not so oppressive, not today. The morning was fresh. Again the streets were covered with a white dusting that usually perplexed her. This morning she took in the sights and sounds as if seeing them for the first time. Today she felt there was a way out of this place. Then she stopped to feel the sun on her face.

As she stood at the corner of Maryland and Liberty, Eileen felt as if she was a part of it all.

She realized that Curtis's Famous Weiners was just a block away. While that was not where she had expected to go on this early Saturday afternoon, it was one of her and Joanne's favorite places. Family owned, Curtis' was a very welcoming place. Algea greeted Eileen with a warm smile as Eileen barely stepped inside the door.

"Eileen!"

The sound of Algea's voice saying her name always made Eileen smile. Today, Eileen was already smiling.

"How are you Eileen?" asked Algea.

"Wonderful!" replied Eileen.

"Here. You sit here where you can watch the world go by," said Algea directing Eileen to a table where she could sit and face the street. "What will you have today?"

"Two hot dogs, French fries, and a chocolate milk shake," Eileen stated clearly as she folded her hands on the table like a school girl. Algea took down her order and disappeared around the counter. Eileen was soon lost in her thoughts. She smiled feeling as she had longed to feel, as a woman with him still lingering within her.

She sighed as she whispered, "FR." *I wonder what he's doing right now.*

THE WALK

After Mass, Frank pulled on his sweater, touched his shirt pocket to be sure his cigarettes and Zippo were in place. *FR* he thought to himself and smiled. He had become used to hearing her call him FR.

He stepped out onto the sidewalk and surveyed the new day of this new year, January 1946. Standing there, like a soldier conducting a drill, he placed a cigarette in his mouth. His Zippo was out, flipped open, thumbed, to and from the cigarette, and closed again in one swift motion. Task completed, his Zippo back in his pocket, he took a long drag then a second and stood alone in the Cumberland morning.

He turned away from the rectory and walked. He walked often. He strolled from the church's walk to the edge of the sidewalk along the street that brought people to St. Patrick's. He smiled remembering the words of some long lost lecture from the seminary on the meaning of love and how—as a priest— he would be in the world, but not of it. He stood at the edge of the sidewalk that brings the people from the world to him and him down to the world that he is supposed to be in, but not part of.

I can't believe I will be celebrating my fifteenth year as a priest in May he thought to himself.

A train whistled and his thoughts turned to her and the night of their first appointmen. He wondered if the train was en route to Pittsburgh or somewhere beyond. He turned and walked back into the rectory.

After coffee and juice and another Camel he went to his office to pick up a book, *The Baltimore Catechism*.

The walk to the school took only two minutes, enough for one more cigarette. Once inside, he entered the room that was waiting for him. As the children stood to greet him, he smiled broadly and looked about the group as if looking for someone. He saw that she was there.

"Please be seated," he said softly. Most of the children appeared glad to see him.

"Now, let me see, where were we?" asking to see if any of them remembered.

"We were talking about sin," a small voice from the middle of the room reminded him.

"Yes," the priest responded, "Sin. What are the two types of sin?"

Among the group of almost thirty, there are more than a few hands raised. He surveyed those who had their hands raised and those who looked down. He focused in on one of the sets of hands folded neatly on her desk.

"Young lady," he said clearly to the room causing several of the girls to look at him asking, pointing their small hands at themselves as they mouthed aloud, "Me?"

"Young lady. Do you know the two types of sin?" he asked a girl whose hands remained neatly folded in front of her

"Me?" she said pointing her hand to her chest.

"Yes. What are the two types of sin?" he asked again.

"Venial and Mortal, father," she said somewhat shyly.

"Very good. Very good. You are Joanne. I remember you from the last time I was here. Did I get your name right?" he asked.

"Joanne, Father. Joanne Hamilton," she explained reluctantly, knowing that he knew her. Then, as he went on to talk about the occasions of sin and the conditions for a sin to be mortal, she allowed his voice to fade away but remained focused on his face.

It was not so long ago and school had let out early for some unknown reason. Joanne had gotten to the apartment and, as usual, the front door was unlocked. She bolted in and was through the living room and stopped, as if by a wall. There, in her mother's bedroom, in her mother's bed was her mother and...she did not want to believe what she was seeing, Father Frank, this same Father Frank who pretended not to know her.

Things were better between them now, at least he thought so. It was his idea that when he came into her classroom and she did not know the answer to one of his questions, she would raise her hand. If she did know, she would fold her hands on her desk.

Joanne still remembered that afternoon. Upon discovering her mother and the priest in bed she turned and ran, retracing her steps through the apartment and out onto the street. She remembered running down the street. Her rage and tears caused her to stumble and almost fall. Soon her mother was coming up behind her, holding her coat closed. Joanne saw her, but did not know whether to run faster or to fall.

"Joanne...Joanne!" her mother's voice grew louder as it got closer.

"Stop. I want to talk with you," Eileen pleaded as she reached for her little girl. Finally, Eileen grabbed hold of her as she slowed down from the tears and the pain that swelled up inside her.

Sobbing tears more of rage than of sorrow, the little girl allowed her mother to pull her close and hold her.

"I hate you! I hate you!" Joanne screamed. "You're a whore!"

The words pierced Eileen and silenced both of them for what seemed an eternity. Eileen pulled her closer to try to absorb her pain, their pain.

Eileen and Bill had separated several months earlier, soon after the day he went to Pittsburgh and she went to the movies. They decided it was best for Joanne to stay with her mother. So, she did. She visited her Dad often and on more than a few occasions, he took her to Pittsburgh. There they stayed in a hotel that opened onto a big street and was within walking distance of Kaufman's, a department store that Joanne loved to walk to with her Dad. She quietly thought to herself how much her mother would have enjoyed walking through the various floors of beautiful things.

After that day, the day of Joanne's discovery, things were different. Joanne called her father and went to live with him, but only for a while. She missed her mother and loved her and came to terms with a fact of life. Her mother was still her mother, despite this part of her, which she did not like. Within a month mother and daughter were back together in the apartment that Joanne had fled, but things between them would never be the same.

Father Frank had been at her house before. Father Frank, now that she thought about it, was at her house a lot. In fact, Father Frank had been to her house even before her Dad moved out.

She could not like him. She did not even try. She even stopped liking church. She still went with her class and with her mother on Sundays and holy days, but quietly she always prayed that Father Frank would not be the one saying the Mass.

Joanne never really liked him. She remembered the time she, her mother and Father Frank drove to Bedford on a Sunday afternoon for lunch. It was Joanne's birthday and her mother wanted to take her out to celebrate. And that would have been fine, but *he* was there when her father dropped her at her mother's apartment.

Sitting in the back of Father Frank's spacious black Buick, she stared out the window and tried only to listen to the radio and not to their conversation, which, despite it all, was pleasant. They seemed to like each other. They did not yell like her mother and father had been doing right before the break-up. She almost felt comfortable, at home, and probably would have been had it not been for the fact that the man her mother was having such a nice time with was a priest.

They arrived at the restaurant and once inside, sitting at a table that gave them a view out over the spring blossoming trees of western Pennsylvania, Eileen, as was her habit, observed "Look, there it is, our piece of the world. Wouldn't it be nice to be able to go and see the rest of it?"

"Would you like to do that?" the priest asked Joanne.

Wondering if he or her mother even cared what she thought, Joanne replied, "I only want to get out of Cumberland."

"What do you mean by that?" asked Eileen testily.

"Didn't you say you want to go and see the rest of it?" Joanne shot back.

"Yes, but you sound as if you don't like Cumberland," said Eileen searching for some help to explain her daughter's comment. These thoughts—Eileen's thoughts captured in her daughter's words—troubled her.

"Only part of it," Joanne mumbled as she picked up her menu to hide her face.

As they were finishing their lunch and Eileen was taking the last sip of her second Tom Collins, the waitress approached with two dishes. One was filled with ice cream topped with fudge, whipped cream, and a cherry. The other held a lit candle on a cupcake.

"Happy Birthday to you," the waitress sang as Eileen and FR joined in. "Happy Birthday to you…"

Joanne smiled reluctantly and blew out the candle.

Gradually, grudgingly, Joanne began to eat her sundae. Father Frank reached down and pulled up a box neatly covered with purple wrapping paper. He offered it to the young lady who was now lost in her ice cream sundae.

"Joanne," Eileen prodded her.

"Thank you," came Joanne's empty words.

"You are welcome," said Father Frank. "I hope you like it."

Taking the box, Joanne was careful to move the sundae just out of the way, not out of reach. She placed the box on the table and lifted the lid. Lifting first one piece of tissue then the second, she stared at the contents. Eileen reached over to pull the contents from the box.

"Isn't that pretty?" Eileen smiled as if what she was looking at was hers. There between the layers of white tissue was a pleated skirt and a white blouse.

"What do you say?" said Eileen looking for some sort of courtesy from her daughter. "It's very nice, Father," Eileen said for Joanne.

Joanne went back to her sundae.

That night, back in their apartment, Joanne tried to drown out her mother's lighthearted voice on the phone with the priest by listening to her favorite radio shows. Unable to do so, she went to her room. From beneath her bed she slowly removed the box. Placing it on the bed, she lifted the contents, laid them out on top of the box. She walked to her desk. Returning to the box with a pair of scissors she proceeded to slowly and methodically chop the skirt into strips.

Her mother never asked her to wear the outfit. One day, about a month later, Eileen was tidying-up Joanne's room and she came across the box. She remembered the ride and the lunch and the gift. She sat it on the bed. Lifting the lid, remembering how pretty it was she pulled back the tissue paper. Raising the skirt to admire it, she held it higher and farther away. It was then she noticed the strips. Her anger turned to tears. She sat down on the bed and, pulling the ruined skirt to her face, wondered what was happening to her life.

THE MESSENGER

Eileen and her FR had come to find themselves with each other more and more acting as if no one noticed.

In the shadows of St. Patrick's he would reach out to her waiting hand or hover his fingers over her tongue as he whispered "Corpus Christi" and placed the wafer on her tongue.

The weeks passed almost as quickly as the days. It was February, one year since their night at the movie.

They mastered the meeting. "What time will you finish?" she asked once through the confessional screen.

Where most went to confess their sins, they met to plan theirs. After hearing confessions for more than two hours, he would later find himself confessing to her his struggles with helping so many with their failures to live up to the expectations they believed he held them to. There, in what was once another man's bed, a man to whom she was still married, she now lay with a man who promised to love everyone by not loving only one.

They would meet for one hour or two hours during the day, often on Wednesday afternoon during the time when she had previously gone to the movies. Now, they were the matinee.

People not only talked with one another, some talked with the other priests, even with the Pastor.

"Monsignor, I don't know how to say this," began the story from more than one of the longtime parishioners.

"Say what?" the Pastor simply and politely replied, not wanting to ask.

"Well, Monsignor, I am not the only one."

"The only one?"

"The only one who has seen Father McGowan with Eileen Hamilton. Together. Alone. And Father was not wearing his collar."

"And what?" Monsignor wanted to know.

"It doesn't look right."

Monsignor never agreed or disagreed, only thanked the parishoners for coming forth and assured them that he would look into it. Despite their somewhat awkward relationship, Monsignor liked Frank. He thought he worked hard at being a priest even though he did not always agree with his ideas about how things were to be done.

"Look into it," he repeated to himself. "I guess I will look into it."

I live with the man. I seldom see him when he is not whistling. And his sermons, I am always hearing good things about his sermons. Lately, his sermons are even better. Most who request to see a priest ask for an appointment with Father McGowan. People are always telling me about Father McGowan's inspiring words, his touching messages. He understands. He talks as if he has lived their lives.

Monsignor shook his head and mumbled, almost aloud, *If they only knew...if they only knew the struggles we, their priests, wrestle with.*

As Monsignor pondered what to do about the rumors and his priest, he thought back to a time, a moment when a young lady had caught his eye from the altar. He had not been ordained more than a year and she approached him after Mass one day. She reached out to shake his hand and as he clasped hers, he noticed how soft and warm it was. And as she thanked him, more with her eyes than with her barely audible words, for his wonderful sermon, he felt the warmth of more than just her hand.

He turned and blushed as the young lady said, "You make the Gospel stories come alive for me."

It was the first time someone complimented him on a homily.

He remembered how much that touched him and how the two or three times they met and talked again were moments of good conversation and communion. But he also knew where to draw the line, which to him was not as imaginary as it might have been to others. To him it was real and he did not ever consider crossing it.

Now, what to do about Father McGowan?

Reluctantly, he decided to contact the Archbishop. He began the letter:

Your Excellency:

I hope this finds you in God's grace and that your health is back. (He had heard that the Archbishop's gout had been acting up, so much so that he had not been able to participate in confirmations).

As you may remember, it was almost two years ago that you assigned Father McGowan to me here at St. Patrick's.

A knock on his office door drew Monsignor from what he was doing. He did not get back to the letter that day. Later, he could not remember whether or not he ever sent it or even finished it. Meanwhile, most everyone in town seemed to be in on the rumors, some choosing not to see anything and others telling anyone who would listen about the gossip. It was a source of energy for this town where the dreariness of the week's work seemed a little less so with the story about the priest and the lady who, as far as anyone there knew, was still married. The only other thing that captured the attention and energy of so many in this town tucked away from the world had been the war which, for most, was over.

It was a Tuesday. A strange car drove down Eileen's street. Eileen happened to look out the window as it parked. She was surprised to see two men in military uniforms get out and walk to the house across the street.

I wonder why they are here? she asked herself, not thinking much about it as she prepared to leave. She was so preoccupied with where she was going, she hardly had time to think much about the uniformed visitors.

She had not been feeling well. Thinking she might be having a relapse of her stomach problems that had put her in the hospital a year and a half ago, she had called and made an appointment to see Dr. Carr. Slowly she walked down the street past the house where the car was parked and the two soldiers had entered. Trying to remember who lived there, she did remember seeing a young boy, maybe 17 or 18 in a uniform last summer. If her memory served her right his name was Robert John Lee. She felt good that she could remember his name, but did not dwell on it as she increased her pace to get to her appointment on time. She tried not to think about what might be the reason for the soldiers' visit.

There were only two people in the waiting room when she arrived at the doctor's office. Small with only four chairs and a table with a lamp and one or two *Life* magazines, Eileen, trying not to be noticed, smiled briefly at the strangers and soon hid her face behind a magazine. In less than a minute she closed the magazine, refusing to look at any more pictures of war and death.

"Eileen," rose a voice as the door opened to reveal a rather old looking man with a bow tie and stethoscope hooked to his neck holding a folder in his left hand.

Dr. Carr was still tall, despite the fact that his shoulders had already begun to hunch from all of life's illnesses he had borne with his patients. As he closed the door behind Eileen, he asked her to be seated and moved slowly through the niceties that doctors use to calm nervous patients. It was his way to take a patient's temperature without a thermometer.

"How's Joanne?" he asked as he listened closely to hear how Eileen answered the question.

"Fine," Eileen said. "She's fine."

Her eyes wandered about the cluttered room to the even more cluttered oak roll top desk covering most of the wall beneath the framed picture of Dr. Carr's family. The office looked like a Norman Rockwell painting.

"And Bill, how is Bill?" he asked matter of factly, knowing that things had not always been okay with them. He was there to deliver Joanne, and remembered the mixture of laughter and tears the young couple shared when their first child was born just shy of nine months after their marriage.

"Well," she said hesitatingly, her eyes looking down into her lap where her hands clutched a handkerchief. "Bill and I are separated."

She was relatively sure that he had already heard the news. She struggled to hold back tears. Sitting silent, she waited for him to speak, hoping he would move on to talk about something else.

"I am sorry to hear that," Dr. Carr said, reaching out and touching her hand as his eyes tried to reassure her.

"What brings you here today?"

"Well, it's my stomach," she began and went on to explain how she had been nauseated and thought it might be some of the old problems.

"Please slip off your dress and put this gown on," instructed Dr. Carr. "You can step behind that screen over there. Have you missed a period?"

"Well, yes," she said reluctantly.

"When was the last time you and Bill...?"

"Some time ago," she interrupted his sentence.

Realizing this made her even more nervous, he tried to ease her.

"There has been a stomach virus going around. So, as soon as you are ready, we can check."

"Pregnant. I can't believe I'm pregnant," she kept repeating to no one but herself.

In a daze she made her way back through the empty streets of Cumberland, pulling her coat up against her neck as the March wind seemed more piercing than usual. So preoccupied was she that she did not even remember the strange car with soldiers from earlier that day. Now that car had been replaced with another, FR's.

He usually doesn't drive down the street. He usually parks around the corner, or walks, she thought to herself. As she opened the door, she noticed FR coming out of the house across the street. Trying not to look obvious, she pushed her front door almost shut and stood and watched as he got in his car and drove away.

Once inside, Joanne came bolting through the tiny rooms and threw her arms around her mother's waist.

"And how was your day?" Eileen said as she returned the hug noticing how tall her daughter had become.

Eileen's emotions took over. As she hugged her not-so-little girl she felt a rush of feelings ranging from excitement to despair.

"What's wrong Mommy?" Joanne asked.

"Oh, nothing. I'm just glad to see you," Eileen said as she started to cry.

"Then, why are you crying?"

"Sometimes people cry when they're happy. So, how was your day?' she asked to shift the topic.

"Okay, I guess."

"I guess? Why do you have to guess if your day was okay?'

"Well, sometimes I don't like school."

"I thought you liked school?"

"Did you like school, Mommy?"

One of those awkward questions, a question that she found herself looking for a way around. She decided to answer.

"I can remember not wanting to go to school…."

As Eileen watched Joanne listen to her tell of a time or two when she did not like school, she continued to notice how her little girl was growing up. Then she listened as Joanne went on about the trials of being thirteen years old and learning how to come to terms with teachers who bored her with their endless lessons and boys who bothered her by pretending not to notice her or talk to their friends about her as if she was not even there. Eileen enjoyed these moments with her first child as she pondered the future of her second child now within her.

For now, Eileen wanted this moment to go on for at least a while knowing that it would end much too soon. To keep it going she prepared a plate of cookies and a glass of milk for each of them. As she brought in the plate and glasses of milk she thought, *I guess I will need to be drinking more of this.* The two sat there for one of the last times it would be just the two of them.

Soon, Joanne was asking to go out to play for a while before dinner. Reluctantly the mother let her child go. As Eileen stood up from the couch, her thoughts swirling around the new life inside her, she looked out to notice more than the usual number of cars on the street. Coming back to reality, her wonder turned to fear, fear that the war had come to her street. She walked to the kitchen and turned on the radio, looking for something to take her away. She busied herself with making dinner rather than allow any more thoughts of what actually might have happened. It was during the news that she learned that Marine Private First Class Robert John Lee of Cumberland, Maryland, died from wounds he had received six months earlier in the Pacific.

Not sure she even wanted to see him, she went about her usual Wednesday ritual of taking a mid-day bath and choosing something nice to wear. She was not sure, but when he came to the door all ambivalence vanished.

"You look more radiant than usual today," he observed as he stepped back to gaze into her eyes after a kiss hello.

She looked down and then at him—straight into his eyes.

"I'm pregnant," she said with tears following her words.

Silence.

"Pregnant?" he asked as if he did not hear her words clearly. He used a tone he might use with one of his catechism class students struggling with an answer.

"Yes. I'm pregnant."

"Are you sure?"

"I wasn't. Didn't even think about it until I went to the doctor's."

"The doctor? Why did you go to the doctor?"

"To find out why my stomach has been upset for the last week or so."

By now he had found his way to the couch and was lighting a cigarette. It was as if his Zippo was a beacon to help him find the way. She turned and watched him go through this ritual in a new, unfamiliar way.

"Are you alright?" she asked

"Yes," he replied looking up to see her standing over him. "'Are *you* alright?' is the question."

He stood and directed her to sit down.

"Yeah, I'm fine," she sighed. "Now I know why I have been feeling so sick in the morning."

Sitting down beside her, the two just sat there for the longest time waiting for words.

"Don't worry, Frank, this will be alright," she said trying to reassure him.

"We'll get married," he almost blurted out while looking straight ahead into the haze of smoke into which he wanted to disappear. It was as if he was trying to convince himself more than her. She, who wanted nothing less, was already hesitating, more for him than herself.

"Frank," she started, "that would be nice, but..." her words began to trail off as she stared at her hands in her lap.

"What is it?" he asked, looking to her for an answer.

"I don't think it would work."

"Why not?"

"Frank, you're a priest. Priests don't get married."

"Eileen, do you hear what you're saying? I know priests are not supposed to get married, nor are they supposed to..."

Interrupting, she began aloud, "What do you think we should do? I love the idea of having your baby and yet I know you are a priest, a priest more than anything."

Her voice trailed off into tears. He reached over to touch her, hesitating, half afraid she would push him away. Before they knew it they were in her bed, actually now more their bed. The comfort of their bodies helped manage the complexities. Almost as if their togetherness, which had been such a source of ambiguity, was now the remedy for them.

"I do want to marry you, be with you the rest of our lives," said Frank.

Their passion brought out his words as easily as the other elixirs he imbibed.

"Not yet," she told him. "Not yet, not now. Let's wait. First, I have to have the baby. I will have to go away."

"Where will you go?"

"I don't know. A couple years ago the Adams girl got pregnant. She went somewhere. I think to Pittsburgh. She had the baby...and she came back."

Shyly, she looked at him. "In fact, I think one of the priests helped her.'

"I think I know who," he admitted. "There is a group of nuns in Pittsburgh who have a home. A home..."

She put a single finger to his lips asking him not to speak any more words. She tried not to think of anything else as they lay there in the day lit room. She only wanted the comfort he provided her, now.

"To know that you love me is enough for right now," she whispered. "We'll figure out what to do when we need to, in time."

Eileen drifted off to sleep, there in Father Frank's arms on a Wednesday afternoon in Cumberland, Maryland.

THE WAIT

The train ride was just a little over three hours. It only seemed like a lifetime. The path was washed with more than a few tears. Eileen gazed out of the window at the passing of the place she had longed to escape. Now her dream turned to a nightmare as the train carried her away from the few tearful goodbyes offered by her sisters and Joanne. She told her daughter that she had to go to a hospital in Pittsburgh to see a doctor who was going to help figure out what was causing her unclear medical condition. Soon she and the space around her were filled with a silence that even the wheels of the train could not pierce. The rolling motion of the train numbed her more.

The panoramic views of the rolling Appalachians that connected Maryland to Pennsylvania would have typically brought a smile to her face. Not today. She felt stuck between two states, somewhere between there and him, then and now. As the train neared Pittsburgh, she hardly noticed how the day had become as grey and bleak as her mood. Pennsylvania Station was not far from where she would go to stay, to wait.

Rosalia Foundling Home was just on the edge of downtown, next to the Hill District, where the Negroes lived, a few blocks from Fifth Avenue. Ironically, Rosalia was also not far from the Sheraton Hotel where she and Bill honeymooned to celebrate their marriage.

Two of the sisters from Rosalia were on their way to meet her. The elder nun drove a black Buick as if she had been doing it all her life. Actually, she had. Her father had owned a Buick when she was still at home. She drove when the family took her to enter her first year. Called the Novitiate, it was a year designed to test her will, help her explore whether or not she really had a vocation. Although she had often thought about leaving, she stayed. And now, ten years later, she was the "senior" of the pair coming to pick up another of their "girls," as they called them.

Although, this time, their passenger would be a bit older than most of the other "girls."

Sister Mary Theresa and Sister Cecelia, the younger of the pair, looked about for a parking space. Sister Mary Theresa was already sizing up a spot when Sister Cecelia shouted, "There's one!"

"Yes, Sister, I see," she said trying to calm, but not quell, her excitement.

Eileen stood on the sidewalk outside the station not sure whom to expect, only to be sure to have a Miraculous Medal pinned on her coat. The two Sisters approached Eileen as if they were old friends. They always directed their "girls" to pin a Miraculous Medal with a blue and white ribbon on their coats. That way they could approach them with a degree of familiarity.

"Hello," said the elder of the two women. "Eileen? I am Sister Mary Theresa and this is Sister Cecelia."

Nodding yes and attempting a smile, Eileen absently pulled her coat around her slightly protruding belly.

"Welcome to Pittsburgh," said the younger, rosy cheeked woman who seemed happy to be out and about on this mission. "Let me take your bag."

Eileen was relieved to have someone to be with.

"Is this your first time in Pittsburgh?" asked the younger woman as she and Eileen hurried to try and keep up with their leader who quickly made her way through the sparse jumble of arrivers and collectors.

Their car was parked not far from the station door and Eileen barely had time to register the cityscape as the elder pointed out the Buick. It was just like FR's, Eileen thought. Her heart sank and her brief moment of relief passed. She was back in her memories of her times in the city together with Bill. She started to sob, and had to stop and collect herself. The younger sister stepped toward her not quite realizing what was going on.

"Are you okay?'

"Yes, Sister, I'll be fine. There's a lot going through my head right now."

The elder sister watched as the young Sister Cecelia comforted Eileen and helped her into the car. Carefully closing the door, the younger sister moved to the back door and took her place in the seat behind Eileen.

As the car pulled away from the station and onto the not too crowded street with its business people and shoppers, Eileen sat back and slowly turned to look out the window, somewhat in awe of all that she saw. The tall buildings and stores filled with pleasing sights of dresses and clothes and furniture only made her go back to her memories. Her curiosity and escape turned to sadness.

"Is this your first time in Pittsburgh?" asked the younger sister before remembering she had already asked without receiving a response.

"Not really," she began, but paused to prevent herself from saying *My husband and I...* "I came here a few years ago for a weekend."

With this, Sister Mary Theresa shot a silencing gaze in the direction of young Sister Cecelia, who recognized the signal not to press for further information, if only to be friendly.

Eileen's sense of herself was so slight that she interpreted most any word as an assault on her person. It only sent her deeper into herself. She longed to be alone. She was always seeking more distance, more disconnection from the world she struggled so hard to be a part of.

Although not much past mid-day, it was almost dark. Eileen was surprised to see the street lights come on as the threesome made their way through Pittsburgh. The company of the women comforted her. The bustle of the traffic and the lights both eased her and disturbed her. It all reminded her of FR and those thoughts saddened her.

For it was with FR that the lights were always brighter. She remembered how he used to love to walk the streets and tell her how the bustle of the brightly lit streets fed his soul.

She wondered what he was doing on this Wednesday afternoon as she made her way to her respite where she would wait to deliver their child.

"Well, here we are," said Sister Mary Theresa proud of delivering another of her "girls."

Although the yard seemed much too small to accommodate her Buick let alone the other two already parked, Sister had no difficulty moving the large black car past one car and into a space that waited for her. Eileen looked out the window at the path that led from the busy street to this quiet cavernous refuge, so grey

and dark that Eileen found herself gasping as the car pulled into its
space to park. The building's red bricks were dusted almost brown
by the years of soot that the nearby mills generated. The soot was
the by-product of the steel that produced the jobs that put the
bread on the tables and suffocated the lungs of so many.

THE RETREAT

The routine of her waiting place seemed to fit Eileen, its newest resident. After a day or two of staying away from the others, Eileen soon began to enter into the table conversations. While she was not skilled at sewing or some of the other skills the others had, she tried, for a while, to become a part of it all.

The sisters, in particular, impressed her. These women dedicated their lives to helping others. They seemed to be actually joyful. They went about their day's work with a certain joy, almost smiling. Eileen picked up on this behavior. She wasn't quite sure what it was, but she knew something was different about this place. These women never judged her. Her mood began to lighten.

Maybe it was the new life in her. Whatever it was, she was glad for it until one Sunday while she was at Mass. She often thought about FR when she was at Mass, but this morning, as she stood with the others to greet the priest, she actually thought it *was* him on the altar about to say the Mass. He looked enough like him to cause her to think it was him. It was all she could do to get up and slowly walk out of the chapel before one of the sisters, Sister Mary Theresa, joined her.

"Are you okay?" the nun asked.

From behind her tears she assured the sister that all was okay and asked if she might be left alone. Seeing her state, the sister told her that she would check on her after Mass.

"Eileen, it is highly unusual for someone in your condition to leave us," said Sister Mary Theresa to Eileen seated across from her. "You have only been with us for less than two months and you will be delivering in less than three months."

"I understand Sister," Eileen replied, "but I am so uncomfortable here."

"You were doing so well. After your first few days you seemed to be adjusting."

"I was," Eileen said. "Only now I…I don't know what it is, only that I am, I have to find some other place." Her voice trailed off into tears.

"I understand Eileen."

"No you don't!" retorted Eileen. "You have never had to."

"How do you know what I have or have not had to do?" asked Sister Mary Theresa.

This stopped Eileen. She sat looking at the sister and realized that she did not know much about her life and what she may have had to do.

"Eileen, all of us have trials. We all have difficulties to face. And while each is different and unique, they are ours. The secret, or better put, the way through them is to accept them and allow others to accompany you, as we are here to do."

Sister Mary Theresa stopped and waited for the words to get to Eileen, and hopefully, for her to hear them.

THE ROOM

It was a clean room, a small room. There on the third floor of a very large house in Squirrel Hill.

Eileen had found it in the newspaper, *Room to rent. Help with school age children and some cleaning and light cooking.*

At first Eileen thought about not telling them she was pregnant. But her thin frame could not hide her condition. Freida Klein, the woman of the house, liked Eileen. Perhaps it was Eileen's ability to make sadness attractive or because she reminded Freida of her sister who had died a few years earlier while giving birth. So, despite her reservations about Eileen being pregnant, she agreed to let her stay. Soon the children became attached to her and actually began calling her "Aunt Eileen."

Eileen had become a part of the family. She made sure the children were dressed and ready for school. Mr. Klein always drove them to school in the morning even though he was usually not home from the family's restaurant until after 1:00 AM. He said it was his special time with his children.

Eileen did the laundry and cleaned and prepared the evening meal two nights a week. The other nights they ate at the family restaurant. Eileen was always invited to join them. Sometimes she did. And while this routine brought with it some sense of well being, Eileen still fell victim to bouts of depression and wanted to be back home in Cumberland with Joanne and FR.

She called Joanne every Sunday evening. Bill dropped Joanne off at Mary's on Sunday afternoon because he would go out of town on business first thing Monday morning. On Sundays the Klein family spent the day together on trips to the movies or the museum and then ate at the restaurant, so Eileen had the house to herself. All day she waited for the call. The anticipation filled her with a certain joy. All day she would think of the things she wanted to say to Joanne. Joanne always asked how she was feeling and when the doctors would make her better so she could come home.

Joanne always waited anxiously near the phone. As soon as she heard Aunt Mary say, "Yes I will accept the charges," she rushed to take the phone from her.

"Hello. Joanne? Is that you? This is mommy."

All of what they were going to say faded away as the two fought back tears. The calls always ended too soon and Eileen would find herself with a list of things she didn't say. "I'll just tell her next week."

Her Sunday night was over yet it was just past six o'clock. Sometimes she would listen to the radio, read the Sunday paper, or, on the nice evenings, which were becoming more frequent, she would walk. She loved to walk. The streets were tree lined with well kept lawns and often there were many walkers out.

On one such evening she met a woman about her age. Eileen had set out to the local ice cream store pre-occupied with the thought of a chocolate ice cream sundae. Almost there, another block to go, a young woman came up along side of her as she waited for the light to change.

"Is this your first?" the lady asked.

A bit startled by the unsolicited comment, Eileen nodded her head.

"Yes," she replied, realizing how pregnant she really looked.

"I would love to have children. My husband and I have been trying."

"Oh, I am sorry," Eileen said as she thought, *Some people have all the luck.*

"Now he is in a hospital in Boston," the woman continued without a nod from Eileen.

"In Boston?" Eileen asked acknowledging the woman's comment.

"Yeah. He was wounded at Iwo Jima over a year ago."

"Iwo Jima?"

"Yeah, that's what I wondered when I read the letter. It's an island in the Pacific. He's a Marine."

"Oh."

"Yeah. He's a crazy Marine. Really didn't have to go. He's the oldest guy in his group. They call him Pops he's so old."

With a smile, Eileen turned to her and the two started out onto the street as she observed, "Pops. That's kind of cute."

Once across the street, Eileen turned to the left to make her way past the stores to her destination. The stranger continued to walk with her. When Eileen turned into the ice cream store, the stranger turned with her.

"Looks like we're going to the same place," said the stranger.

Eileen was not quite sure what had happened but there the two sat, she eating her chocolate ice cream sundae and her new friend enjoying a banana split. The woman talked about how much she missed her husband. She shared with Eileen how she was going to Boston to visit her husband.

She told Eileen about her sister and the landlady where she lived. "If it weren't for the two of them, I don't know how I would make it."

Eileen enjoyed listening to her talk with such love and joy about these people that were in her life. How important they all were to her. It reminded her of her family and, inevitably, FR.

The two sat and talked after they finished their ice cream treats and soon they were both on their separate ways back to their respective homes. It was then that the idea of someone adopting her baby came to her.

Back in her room Eileen closed the door. She reached into the drawer beside her bed and pulled out a small stack of letters wrapped with a single piece of purple ribbon.

FR knew where Eileen was. Eileen had sent her address to him and he wrote often. It was his letters that kept him alive for her. There was a new one that arrived the day before that she had saved.

> Eileen,
>
> It is Saturday night and I just finished writing my sermon for tomorrow. Fortunately, I have the two later Masses so I will be able to sleep a little longer. And that is good because I am going to a parishioner's for dinner.
>
> I only wish that you would be sitting across the table from me. Your beautiful smile lights up the room and I so enjoy listening to you laugh. Your zest for life is contagious and sometimes very much needed here in the rectory, and more often in the church as a whole.

So many people come to church so burdened. And while some struggle with being stuck in relationships they don't know how they got into (what alcohol and sex won't cause people to do)...*she put the letter on her lap and soon her laugh turned to tears*...others struggle with being alone.

I am arranging to come to Pittsburgh to be with you. *Again, she put the paper down and was very still...he's coming here!*

I have made a decision. I want to live my life with you. Life with you is more alive and more filled with joy than my life here with all of these people who seem only to want something they think they can only get through someone else or after they die. It had been so easy to believe the words I had come know so well and so thoroughly. But, then when I met you everything changed. The words were words and with you they became, real, as it says in the scripture, *et verbum carnum factum est* (and the word became flesh).

I know that many of my brother priests have come to terms with living alone. I thought I had. But, now, well now, everything is a struggle, not that it was easy before. Now it is a struggle with what I should be doing with my life and who I should be struggling with. That is you.

As soon as I am sure when I am coming I will let you know.

All my love,
Frank (FR)

She lay down on the bed with the letter clutched to her swelling breasts and she lay there for the longest time.

105

Sounds of laughing children bouncing up the stairs woke her.

"No, do not knock on her door," Freida's ordered, "I am sure Eileen is asleep."

Sitting up in bed she debated whether to go to the door. Instead, she curled up, letter in hand, and fell back asleep.

THE BLUFF

She stayed with the Klein family waiting for FR to arrive. Every day she anticipated his arrival. Each of her days would end with her holding another of his letters to her breast. She loved him. And she believed he loved her.

In his room he would sit or kneel alone in the empty church. He thought he would receive an answer if only he prayed. He knew he loved her. He knew he wanted to be with her, felt more of a man with her. But there was something about being a priest he could not separate himself from. It was what the church told him. Priests were called to something higher, holier. He had actually believed it for so long. But now, now he was not sure. But for whatever reason, he stayed there at St. Patrick's where he was Father Frank.

More and more she felt less and less sure of what was going to happen. It was then she decided to return to Rosalia Foundling Home. Rosalia was both a place for unwed mothers and a place where mothers could place their babies temporarily while they decided if they would keep them or put them up for adoption.

"Eileen, how good to see you," Sister Mary Theresa said greeting her at the home's door. She escorted Eileen to her office and made two cups of warm tea. Settling down behind a wooden desk, Sister said, "So, tell me, why have you returned?"

"I need a place for my baby," she said, pausing for some reaction from the sister who sat very still. Sister remained quiet knowing that no words were often better than any words.

The two sat silently for a moment taking occasional sips of tea.

Eileen waited for Sister Mary Theresa to say something.

"I need a place for my baby," she decided to start. "I know it will be safe here at Rosalia. And I am not sure I will be able to keep the baby."

With these words she fought tears she thought were under control.

"I understand," said Sister as she stood and slowly came around the desk and offered Eileen a white handkerchief.

Eileen took the cloth to her face. Her tears softened it.

She never felt the touch of his hand on her swollen belly.

Mercy Hospital was where women from Rosalia delivered their babies. It was up on a hill next to Duquesne University. The area was called the "Bluff" because it caught the best of the cold winter days that the city knew so well.

She delivered alone.

"It's a boy," the nurse whispered to her as she brought him close enough for her to see and to hold.

I will call him Joseph, she thought to herself as she took him from the nurse. *Who will know that is FR's middle name?*

On Friday morning, July 26, 1946, she was back in her room and her Joseph was in the nursery, where he began, they began, their wait.

"May I see him?"

"Let me get him," said the nurse in a white uniform.

As she lay there, holding Joseph, she smiled a smile that would have to last a lifetime. She pulled him close and warmly whispered in a soft, clear voice.

"I love you and I will always love you," and she dried the tear that had fallen on his sleepy face.

With her touch, he opened his big blue eyes and she only hoped that he could hear her as she finished her first conversation with him, "I don't know what is to become of you or me, but for now..."

The nurse returned to take her second born, her first son, back to the nursery.

Eileen went back to the Kleins' house and Joseph went to Rosalia Foundling Home. She told the children that her baby was sick and would have to stay in the hospital for awhile. She visited Joseph as soon as she was able. These mother-and-son visits helped, but they were infrequent and soon, too soon, she was back with the man she hoped loved her as much as she loved her Joseph.

FR had arrived. After several promised arrivals, he finally came to be with her. They took a one bedroom apartment in

Shadyside, a pleasant neighborhood with tree-lined streets not too far from Rosalia. She never questioned why he did not visit their son after he explained that someone might recognize him given Rosalia was a Catholic facility. She once suggested he go in his Roman collar. He said he would think about it.

Eileen was usually okay with the way things were but then she would have periods when she wanted it all settled. She was afraid to have the conversation, a conversation that would too soon replace the pain of unknowing with certain pain. They lived a normal life, of sorts. He would go to work, selling Catholic children's books door to door. And after a while Eileen began to wait tables, but only during the lunch hour. She wanted her afternoons so that she could go visit Joseph. But the afternoons often came and went with her only regretting that she could not get to Rosalia. She struggled with visiting her son, their son, no one's son.

In fact, she was having more and more trouble going because of how difficult it had become to leave him for his father. For a while they seemed to be doing okay, then she noticed Frank becoming more and more distant, sullen. His one or two drinks before and during dinner became three or more before, during, and after...until she stopped counting. He seemed edgy, anxious. He often lost his temper. He was trying to be something he could not be. He missed Mass. He missed all that went with missing Mass, the attention. He missed standing before a crowd sharing his thoughts about what Jesus was trying to say. He missed helping provide direction to others. All the while his life drifted. Every time she tried to talk with him about what she saw and felt, he would talk her out of it.

She told him more than once that she was feeling that she was to blame. She felt that she was the "other woman."

"Frank," she said, "as much as I love you, I do not think I can take you from your first love, the priesthood."

Finally, in desperation, she went to see Sister Mary Theresa at Rosalia.

Sister Mary Theresa had been there for Eileen. She listened to her. She could hear her pain and, though it was difficult, she finally posed the question that Eileen dared not ask, but then was almost relieved to hear.

"Eileen, what are you going to do?" asked Sister Mary Theresa.

"Do? About what?" said Eileen trying not to face the question.

"Eileen," began the Sister, "you seem very unhappy. You and Frank. How are you doing? What is going to happen?"

With this Eileen began to cry.

"I don't know, Sister. I don't know," she said through sobs of tears.

Sister knew there was nothing to do but to sit and offer Eileen her hand and a tissue. There in the silence, a silence that lasted long enough to move from uncomfortable to almost serene, Eileen began to speak.

"I feel like I am the other woman. I feel like I am taking him from someone, some*thing* that he does not want to leave." Her voice raised and grew very assertive. "I feel…I feel like I am taking him from *God*."

Sister sat as she usually did when Eileen began to ramble. Moments passed.

"Eileen," she said at last, "you cannot take from God. God only gives and God expects us to give, too. Frank is a grown man and he has made decisions, as you have. If there are other decisions to be made, my hope is that you would make them together."

111

Their second son was born in April 1948. She only saw him once, once long enough to tell him she loved him as she loved his brother, but not long enough to give him a name. She would leave that to the decision she had made.

They were both to be adopted through Catholic Charities.

She decided that she could no longer stay with Frank. She asked Sister Mary Theresa to contact Frank to tell him her decision. Sister Mary Theresa told Frank that Eileen did not want to see him again and that they would have no more contact. He was to leave her and return to the God from whom she believed she had taken him.

Eileen left the hospital up on the Bluff. Spring was bringing new life to this old city while Eileen struggled to breathe. She felt the spring breeze on her face as she felt her soul dying. Across from the Bluff, there next to Duquesne University, she looked out across the river.

Down and across the river in view of where she stood was a church, a Roman Catholic church attached to a monastery. In the church, near the front, in a pew alone, knelt Father Francis Joseph McGowan, now looking even older than his forty-one years. What was left of his thinning hair was very grey. He wore a plain white shirt and black trousers and both soles of his black shoes were almost worn through. He knelt with his face in his hands. He appeared to be praying.

"I still know the words," he said. " I am just not sure if I understand what they mean or even if I want them to mean anything. I am doing what I was trained to do and tell others to do, all the time, but now I am not sure."

112

He paused, put his face into his hands.

"I do not know what I believe, only that there is nothing else for me to do, except to say the words, to say the words and hope, that by some chance there is that God, that someone will hear them."

His words trailed into a silence that lasted several minutes.

"Here I am, alone, in a place where I should feel at home, and all I feel is…is nothing."

It was in this silence that the memory of her voice came to him, *I cannot take you from your first love, the priesthood.*

He realized, as if for the first time, the truth in her voice. It was her voice that gave life to the words. It was her that made flesh all of what he had learned and talked about. He also realized that he was not able or willing to do anything other than what she had set in motion. As a single tear came to his eye, a church bell rang. He remembered what the bells referred to in the seminary, *Vox Dei*, the voice of God calling. And call expects response.

He rose from his knees, stepped to the aisle, genuflected, walked down the aisle, and reached out to the holy water font. He touched his fingers to the water. He lifted his three fingers to his forehead, his heart, and from his left shoulder to his right shoulder.

As he walked down the few front steps he looked out and across the river up to the Bluff.

The Bluff, he thought, *what a strange name for a place for her to say goodbye to me.*

He would not permit any more thoughts as he walked a few steps along the sidewalk to a parked car. He opened the passenger door and sat down and pulling a Camel from his pocket, motioned to the driver—a young man in khakis, shirt, and light jacket—to go. The ride down the hill, across one of several bridges that connected the various parts of the city, was quiet. Neither man spoke. There was nothing to say, and if there was, neither of them was going to say it.

Soon they were at the train station in midtown Pittsburgh.

As they pulled to the curb, the younger man asked, "Do you want me to come in?"

"No thanks, I'll be alright."

"Do you have enough money? Your ticket?"

"Yes, thank you," Frank said, reaching his hand into his coat pocket to make sure his billfold and ticket were there.

Lifting the elder's suitcase from the trunk, the younger man sat it down and motioned for a porter.

The two shook hands and, as the elder started to walk away, the younger man paused looking for something to say, half hoping the elder would turn to look his way. When he realized he was not going to turn, the younger man got back into the car and drove away.

Inside the train station, the lone traveler followed the porter to the ticket counter.

"Good morning sir," said the neatly uniformed ticket taker.

Looking at the man's ticket, he turned, stretching his right arm, "You will be leaving from Track 2 in one hour."

Putting the ticket back in his pocket, he thanked the man and looked at his watch, "It's only 11:00am," he thought to himself, "I wonder if I can get a cup of coffee." He looked around and saw a neon sign illuminated "BAR." He walked toward it with his one bag, a briefcase in his hand, looking like a man on his way to a business trip.

As he crossed the marble floor, he thought of other times and other marble floors. He remembered his last time here. She had come to meet him. She made a scene fussing over him and, for once, he allowed himself to let her fuss, here far away from the world where no one knew him in a place that he thought the two of them would make theirs. Now he was on his way to Texas.

Archbishop Coyle had found him a place to serve. Frank embraced the idea that a prison would be a good place for him to serve as chaplain, at least for a while.

"Coffee, black," he answered the bartender. What he really wanted was a drink. He could almost taste the Jack Daniels as he sipped the hot black coffee. He dragged heavily on his Camel and, as he exhaled, the now refined smoke carried a sigh that caught him a little by surprise, as he often was by any sign of emotion or feeling.

It was not until the train reached Ohio and was making its way west did he begin to feel anything. Aided by a second, then third cocktail in the lounge car he sat at the window and tried to read his breviary, in vain.

The words had become no more than black letters arranged on white paper. He lit another cigarette and began to lift his drink to take a sip, but put it down. The dark of night was beginning to overtake the train. At first, he seemed to be speeding into the unknown with a conviction that would overcome any darkness. But now night seemed to be coming faster and faster and the darkness began to come with a chill that touched his soul. He pulled his jacket collar closer to his neck in a vain attempt to provide some warmth, some comfort.

"Dinner is now being served in the Dining Car," said the pleasant black man as he moved effortlessly through the car.

He turned and watched the messenger walk on and then followed others to the dining car. The dining car had a simple elegance. The table was covered with a white linen cloth and silver knives and forks straddled a shiny ornate plate topped with a neatly folded white napkin. The small candle was lit by a white gloved black man almost as soon as he sat down.

"Yes," he said with a bit of a smile on his face, he began humming to himself. "Maybe this will make it a little bit better."

As Frank made himself comfortable, the black man stepped close to the table. He looked at him and smiled and asked, "Is that 'Am I Blue' you are humming?"

"Yes," he replied through the bravado of the few cocktails. "Indeed it is and indeed I am."

"Another cocktail sir?" came the voice standing at his side.

"Yes, Jack Daniels on ice with a glass of water on the side," he explained to the nodding face. And, as the man walked to get his drink, Father Francis J. McGowan turned and looked out into the darkness of the spring night.

THE END

Made in the USA
Middletown, DE
07 September 2015